THE MARQUIS WALTZED HER OUT
ONTO THE BALCONY...

There they continued to dance until the music ebbed away. Afterward, Beth remained standing against him for one enchanted moment, her eyes closed.

His hand glided up her arm, tingling across her bare neck and tipping her chin upwards toward him. Before she realised what was happening, his mouth had closed over hers.

The demanding passion of his kiss called forth a longing of her own. Surely she should pull away, cry out, even slap him. But Beth could only do what she honestly wanted to, and that was to twine her arms about his neck and kiss him back with all her h___. Beth found her breath coming quic___

"Yes, you are ___ ___ lordship murmured, bu___ ___ ___ artfully you s___ ___ ou are well pr___

Stu___ ___ stepped back and stare___ ___ dismay. "I have never ..." ___ ___, and then realised he would not ___ the truth, that she had never before allowed a man to hold her in this manner. "Clearly you are determined to despise me, no matter what I do or say," she finished.

Beth forced back the tears and his face remained impassive when he answered her, "I have good reason to do so..."

Also by Jacqueline Diamond

A Lady of Letters

Forthcoming from
WARNER BOOKS

The Forgetful Lady

Jacqueline Diamond

WARNER BOOKS

A Warner Communications Company

All the characters and events portrayed in this story are fictitious.

for Kya

=1=

"NOT LAME, IS SHE?"

The frightened note in Lady Elizabeth Fairchild's voice drew a reassuring grunt from the groom. "Not lame, my lady, I don't think, but I wouldn't want to run her after the hounds, if you take my meaning. She's favouring that leg and I've a mind she's best not ridden hard for a while."

Beth's shoulders sagged but she tried not to show the rush of despair that shot through her. "I'm sure you're right, Sam," she said, running a hand over Daisy's golden flank. "Do you know if there's another mare in Lord Meridan's stable that might suit?"

The groom eyed her balefully. "There's another mare, aye, miss, but suitable? Not to my way of thinking."

Beth's chin came up, her involuntary gesture of defiance whenever an obstacle was placed in her path. "And why not?"

"Too skittish," Sam observed. "Near threw the groom that was exercising her when we arrived this morning."

"But I'm a good rider!" she protested.

He nodded reluctantly. "That you are. But headstrong, my lady, if you don't mind my saying it."

The words were impertinent, but while Beth had learned to play the aristocratic lady whenever her equals were watching, at heart she was still the young child who had once scampered almost unsupervised about her father's estate. To her, Sam and the other servants had been far more a family than her real family could ever be.

"I don't mind your saying what you think, Sam, but I've simply got to have a horse tomorrow," she told him. "What's the mare's name?"

"Fancy." He sniffed disapprovingly.

"What a milk-and-water name for a spirited horse!" Beth agreed. "But I'll have her. And take care with Daisy, will you please?" She gave the horse one last stroke and a carrot before strolling back toward the house.

A crisp breeze reminded her that it was late February, and she huddled inside her bottle-green pelisse. This could well be the last foxhunt of the winter. Soon the season would be upon them and the return to London. . . . She shivered and hurried toward the manor house.

It was in fact a medieval castle, impressive and brooding among its imposing towers, but the moat had long since been filled in, and to Beth's way of thinking, the house was far less intimidating than its owner.

She slipped in through the back entrance, hoping to reach her chamber before her mother discovered her absence. She and her younger sister Hester had been instructed to rest after their journey that morning from near Lenham, but Beth hadn't been able to sleep. She'd noticed Daisy favouring one leg as the horses were led behind the carriage, and tomorrow was of too great an importance for her to ignore so serious a matter.

She reached the end of the hall unobserved, and had closed the door safely behind her before she saw Hester sitting upright in bed, fully awake.

Beth paused and the two girls studied each other wordlessly for a moment. Only a year apart in age, they'd been thrust into competition since childhood, and now they regarded each other warily.

It was a battle Hester had unfailingly won. In addition to being the cherished baby of the family, she possessed lovely pale hair and clear blue eyes that seemed to fascinate everyone she gazed upon. Beth could not help contrasting her own boyish looks, the wiry reddish-brown locks that had a mind of their own and the brown eyes that were so out of fashion just now.

Hester toyed with a strand of blonde hair, watching her sister like a cat about to pounce on a mouse.

"You needn't tell me we were supposed to be napping!" Beth reproved, hanging her pelisse in the wardrobe. "I've been to see about Daisy."

Her sister shrugged delicately, her oval face and perfectly regular features masked with indifference. "You may go where you wish, Lizzie, if you insist on this madness of riding in the foxhunt."

"Lady Frankstone plans to do so as well!" Beth yanked a brush through her rebellious hair. "And you know I prefer to be called Beth."

"Lady Frankstone is an old war-horse and may do as she pleases." Hester slipped one tiny foot out of bed, donning her satin slipper with a natural grace that stirred an unwelcome shiver of envy in her sister. "But I suppose with your reputation, you could hardly do otherwise than go galloping across the countryside with the men. I assure you, you'll never catch *me* riding races in Hyde Park—don't deny it, I've heard enough rumours to be convinced they're true."

To cut off the unpleasant conversation, Beth rang for the maid. It was time to be dressing for dinner, and with a third person in the room, even a servant, her sister would most likely revert to the image of sweetness and charity she displayed to the world.

But it wouldn't last, Beth told herself as she selected a rich velvet brown dress that played up the depth of her eyes.

"That's far too grand for dinner," reproved Hester. "Best save it for a ball."

She was right of course. In matters of fashion and taste, Hester had unerring judgement. Beth replaced the dress and selected a pale yellow silk with tan braiding down the bodice.

Reluctantly, she admitted to herself as she was helped to dress by the maid that she and Hester shared, that she would never be Hester's equal. Nor Mary's either, but their older sister had had the grace to fall in love and marry early in her first season, thus sharply disappointing Lady Fairchild's hopes of having a daughter declared an Incomparable.

Two years later, the previous spring, it had been Elizabeth's turn. She had seen from the start that she would never be a success on conventional terms; she felt far more comfortable in spirited discussion with the gentlemen than simpering and fanning herself on the dance floor.

Beth's throat tightened at the memory of her mother's face after the come-out ball, when despite the politeness of her partners it had been clear that the diamonds of that season did not include Lady Elizabeth Fairchild.

She had failed her mother once again. Somehow, since she was small, Beth had been aware that she was a constant disappointment, despite her best efforts. The wildflowers she eagerly brought her mother were ragged and ill-chosen, while Hester's were arranged exquisitely. Beth always had a stain at her hem, a smudge on her face, or the wrong words on her lips.

And so, a year ago, she had faced the most painful dilemma of her life. Was she to retreat in failure, to become one of those young ladies who sits always at the edge of the ballroom, watching the belles of the season flirt and preen before their suitors? For herself, she would not have minded so much, but she could not face her mother's bitter reaction.

It was, in fact, after hearing of some of the exploits of Lady Frankstone that she had hit upon her plan. She would draw attention to herself through outrageous—although never quite improper —behaviour.

Although by nature she was hesitant to push herself forward, Beth had grimly set about her plan. She challenged a male cousin to an early-morning race in Hyde Park, and won. She sported a daring low-cut gown with a Grecian key pattern about the hem; she drank a bit more ratafia than she should at balls, and giggled and told slightly ribald stories she had overheard her father relating to his friends.

Gradually, it became known about town that Elizabeth Fairchild was a good sport, and a number of gentlemen found themselves quite at ease in her company. If they told anecdotes they would have withheld before another lady, and if they were more likely to slap her on the back than to send her flowers, well, that was the price she paid.

There had been several offers of marriage, but none especially enticing. One gentleman, Louis Chumley, might have been acceptable in his person and breeding but for his unfortunate penchant for gambling too deep.

But Elizabeth had another reason for refusing her suitors. She was in love, hopelessly in love—with the wrong man.

"Lizzie!" Hester, faultlessly gowned in white muslin, snapped her fingers to rouse her sister from her reverie. "That's enough woolgathering. We'll be late for dinner."

Beth trailed Hester downstairs, hearing the voices of the other guests already ringing through the house. Lord Meridan had assembled most of his neighbours and some friends from as far away as London, for this was one of the last major social events to precede the annual return to town.

"Of course she should!" Lady Frankstone was declaring stoutly. "I daresay, I cannot abide a simpering miss! Your daughter, Lady Fairchild, is the only young woman worthy of respect from the last crop!"

Beth quivered inside. They were talking about her, debating whether she should go on the foxhunt as she had insisted. She hated being the topic of conversation, particularly one in which so much criticism was likely to be levelled at her, but she must live up to the reputation she had established for herself.

The moment of hesitation wasn't lost on Hester. As Beth squared her shoulders and forged ahead in the drawing room, a smile teased around the corners of the younger girl's mouth.

She adjusted the skirt of her own demure white dress and followed slowly behind, obviously aware that the contrast between them set her off to advantage.

"The very person!" Lady Frankstone, a portly figure with unnaturally black hair, surged forward and seized Beth's hand, tucking it under her arm. "She shall ride, shan't you, Beth?"

All heads turned toward them. Elizabeth was painfully aware of one particular set of sardonic green eyes, burning in the face of their host himself.

"Of course I shall!" she stated firmly. "But first I must beg a favour of Lord Meridan."

She disengaged herself from her mentor and strode across the room with seeming ease to face the tall and not at all welcoming man who leaned against the mantel.

"My lord, the groom informs me that my mare is injured," she said. "I beg leave to borrow your horse, Fancy."

The coldness of his gaze chilled Beth's nerve, but she refused to back down and stood waiting before him in the self-assured pose she had carefully adopted.

"The horse has a tendency to shy easily," his lordship returned finally. "I fear she might prove difficult to handle."

"But not for me," Beth said.

He shrugged. "That is for your father to decide, Lady Elizabeth. It is of no concern to me." He turned away, almost rudely, to speak to someone else.

Hoping her face didn't reveal her embarrassment, Beth approached her father. The Viscount William Fairchild sat on a sofa beside an elderly lord, deep in a conversation about the training of foxhounds.

"Father," she said. "May I have your permission to ride Lord Meridan's mare, Fancy?"

"Eh? Whatever you wish, whatever you wish," her father responded irritably, and continued his conversation without looking up at her.

Beth caught sight of her mother's disapproving expression. The most frustrating thing of all had been that, although her success had rescued her from failure in society's eyes, Lady Eleanor Fairchild had not been pleased.

Then her mother's gaze touched on Hester and softened. With a twist of her heart, Beth observed the pride that crept into Lady Fairchild's expression as she watched her youngest daughter's lovely face and gracious attentiveness to an elderly duke.

Without half trying, Hester would have everything that Beth had laboured and sacrificed for. And perhaps even everything she had dreamed of.

Beth peered from beneath lowered lashes at the Marquis of Meridan, who still stood by the hearth. He appeared absorbed in listening to a beefy country squire, but how long would it be before he too would notice Hester's beauty and charm?

Going to stand beside Lady Frankstone, Beth stared down at her folded hands. She had first seen the marquis the morning in Hyde Park when she'd raced her cousin, although she hadn't been introduced to him until several days later, at Almack's.

The introduction had almost obligated him to dance with her, and he had done so with frosty politeness. To her dismay, Beth had found herself irresistably attracted to the man, with his sandy hair, almost arrogant self-assurance, and penetrating green eyes.

From then on, she had watched with growing pain as he favoured one lady and then another with his attentions at the balls, routs, and breakfasts that highlighted the season. From time to time she caught him gazing at her, generally with disapproval but sometimes with an expression she couldn't read. Whatever his thoughts, the result was clear: The one lady he never chose to attend was Lady Elizabeth Fairchild.

Although he was their neighbour, she had seen him only two or three times during the winter in Kent, and his attitude toward her appeared to have changed for the worse. Where he had been indifferent before, she sometimes felt now as if she had inspired his deepest distaste. Yet search her memory as she might, Beth could alight upon no reason for such censure.

Soon the new season would start, with its new beauties, especially Hester, who would have her eighteenth birthday in only a week's time. Tomorrow was the foxhunt, and Beth's last chance to shine in a habitat that suited her best, a country estate far from London.

She still harboured the faint hope that he would notice her then, admire her courage and daring, chat with her easily about masculine topics as some gentlemen seemed to enjoy doing.

If she could not spark at least a tiny flame of interest tomorrow, she knew he would be lost to her forever.

At that moment, Hester herself was well aware of the marquis's commanding presence as he leaned against the mantel across the room, but she kept her eyes steadily on the garrulous old duke. In her almost eighteen years, she had learned that she attracted attention best by doing least. Let Beth make a ninnyhammer of herself, gallivanting about London and riding to the hounds; Hester would win out in her own way.

Even as the duke prosed on, Hester covertly watched the marquis's face. His gaze occasionally strayed to Beth, although he seemed to jerk his attention away almost angrily. Somehow her sister had managed to antagonise this most desirable man, no doubt by her hoydenish behaviour.

It wasn't that Hester felt herself in love with the marquis; there was something too stormy and powerful about him to suit her taste. But the goal, after all, was not simply to please oneself. Hester wanted above all to be acclaimed, admired, and envied, and to achieve that position she fully intended to capture the heart and hand of the most eligible lord in England.

Dinner was announced. Lord Meridan, all graciousness, approached and asked to escort Lady Frankstone, who consented with alacrity. He did not look once at Beth as he led the way in to supper.

Beth murmured soothingly to the mare Fancy, who eyed her suspiciously. A palmful of sugar from the kitchen had smoothed their introduction somewhat, but the horse was clearly not an easy-natured beast. Beth, although a strong rider, was not nearly so bold as she pretended, and she had to force herself not to be disheartened at the thought of mounting this possibly dangerous creature.

Lord Meridan rode toward her, pulling his stallion up sharply. "Everyone else is ready, Lady Elizabeth," he informed her. "If the horse frightens you, you needn't join us, but I must ask that you make some decision rapidly."

That was all the challenge she needed. "It is my custom to become acquainted with a horse before I ride it," Beth shot back, and quickly let Sam help her up into the sidesaddle. "I assure you, I am as ready as anyone, my lord."

"Do be careful, Lizzie!" Hester's voice floated across the lawn in front of Meridan Castle. The younger girl was set off to her best advantage by a pale pink muslin morning dress, her fair hair curling about her face.

Only Beth knew that the concern was purely for show; if anything, her sister wished to call attention to Beth's unladylike bravado and her own estimable propriety.

Hester was not really malicious, Beth told herself as she reined Fancy about and joined the other riders. She was merely selfish and spoiled, and not in the way of concerning herself with the needs of others.

The day was pleasantly warm for February, and Beth pushed aside her troubled thoughts as she rode. Fancy seemed to settle down after some initial dancing about, and her rider was able to concentrate on the fresh earthy smell of late winter and the refreshing sight of the men in their black and red hunting jackets.

Lady Frankstone bobbed along somewhere ahead of her, also clad severely in black. Beth had selected a red jacket that called attention to her vivid complexion and bright brown eyes. Her mother had disapproved the colour and its effect, pointing out that ladies of fashion maintained milk-white skin even to the point of employing bleaching creams.

Near the head of the pack rode Lord Meridan. The sight of his broad shoulders and narrow waist sent a pang of longing through Elizabeth.

She must not give up yet! And, hearing the hounds begin to bay, she determined that this was her chance.

The fox had been scented, and the chase was on. Horses surged forward, riders leaning to aid their mounts as they leaped hedgerows and fences.

Beth guided Fancy at a gallop through the midst of the throng, determined to catch up with his lordship. The horse's nervous energy found a welcome outlet in the leaps and mad dashes across fields, and they quickly moved up toward the head of the hunt.

Beyond, she heard the baying deepen and caught sight of a flash of red as the fox fled for its life.

It was Beth's first foxhunt, although she'd often ridden through this countryside alone, imagining herself to be one of the throng. Until she'd come out this past season, she'd never have dared to try to ride to the hounds.

Now the brief glimpse of the little animal ahead striving madly to stay alive struck her painfully and unexpectedly, even as Fancy continued to thrust forward. What a hideous spectacle they must be, these men and women atop their powerful horses, pounding toward a helpless small creature that would soon be torn to shreds by a pack of ravening hounds.

Beth knew almost without giving it conscious thought that even to attempt to interfere with the hounds would be to court disaster. Yet she could not allow this savagery, no matter what it cost her in the repugnance and ridicule of society.

Spurring her horse forward, she had come within half a dozen lengths of the marquis, possibly because as the leader he dodged and veered with the dogs while she was able to make straight toward him. He paid no notice to her or anyone else, intent on the kill to come.

Yes, he too, Beth thought. All of them. The memory of the past year, of her subterfuge and desperate striving for acceptance, welled up in her mouth with a bitter taste. *She* was that fox, running its little heart out and knowing that in the end they would tear it to shreds without a thought.

She no longer cared whether the Marquis of Meridan were impressed by her. How foolish she had been to sacrifice her self-esteem for even five seconds to please these bloodthirsty nobles! Beth lifted her riding crop and brought it down on Fancy's flank.

The touch of the whip seemed to spur the mare to a frenzy. She soared across a fence and thundered past the marquis, who shouted something that was lost to Beth in the rushing wind.

Onward they plunged into the midst of the hounds, who yelped and parted to make way. The houndmaster cried an oath, and Beth, afraid of crushing one of the dogs, tried to rein in her horse. But Fancy had the bit between her teeth now and there was no stopping her. The cold wind slapped at Beth's cheeks and numbed her ears; her throat constricted with fear as her horse ate up the distance across a field toward a high fence.

"Runaway!" she screamed, but if others were trying to catch her up, she couldn't hear them through the pounding of her own blood.

The fence. It was much too high to jump at this point, sitting atop a rise. Panic-stricken, she sawed at the reins, trying to turn the horse, but in vain.

The ground rose and Fancy raced up it, jumping at the last minute. Beth, gripping the mane to stay on the awkward sidesaddle, gasped as they seemed to clear the hurdle.

But not quite. The mare's rear hoofs caught on the top railing. For a frozen second, the horse struggled to regain her balance, then the girl felt herself catapulted earthward.

A blinding flash filled her head, and then nothing.

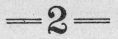

=2=

SHE DIDN'T KNOW where she was when she opened her eyes. Morning light streamed across the bed, and leaning over her was an intensely handsome man with worried green eyes.

"Elizabeth?" he asked as she stirred.

She blinked, becoming aware of a dull ache in her head. Elizabeth. It had a familiar sound to it. Perhaps it was her name.

"Who are you?" she said, her mouth feeling dry and thick as a wad of cotton.

The man frowned. "Brett . . . Lord Meridan," he told her. "Don't you remember me?"

Beth tried to shake her head, and winced. "Where am I? Why . . . why does my head hurt so?" She gazed blearily about her, receiving the vague impression of an austere but elegant bedchamber, with finely made but unornamented oak furniture.

Lord Meridan reached down and wound a lock of her auburn hair around his finger as he gazed at her thoughtfully. "Do you truly not remember the accident? We were riding to the hounds, and the mare ran away with you. I had no idea she was so wild. You've been unconscious the better part of two days."

She searched her memory, but found to her astonishment that it was blank. Her widened eyes must have revealed her horror.

"What is it?" He touched her cheek, and the gesture reassured her inexplicably. "I'm sorry to bring back such painful memories."

"But that's just the problem," she said. "I haven't any. Memories. I can't even recall who I am."

A look of understanding flashed across his high-cheeked face.

17

"It's not uncommon, I've heard, after a blow to the head such as you've received. You'll gain your memory back after a bit, I've no doubt."

Beth smiled, enjoying his nearness and his solicitude. "I have a feeling I shall like that. Are you . . ." She had been about to inquire if he were her husband, but a glance at her own hands warned her that she wore no rings. If not her husband, who was he?

The door opened and an older woman bustled in, her aristocratic face soured by an expression of annoyance. "I declare, I *knew* I heard voices," she stated. "Is my daughter awake then, at last?"

Beth tried to peer more closely at the newcomer, but she didn't look at all familiar and her strident voice rang painfully through Beth's head. "Is she . . . is she really?" she whispered to Meridan and, at his puzzled expression, added very softly, "My mother?"

His nod did little to restore her confidence. For one thing, if she couldn't recognise her own mother and didn't remember this entrancing man, she was in a sorry state indeed. Further, there was something quite forbidding about the lady. She was not at all the tender nurse one would have expected.

"I'm awake," Beth managed to stammer out. "But I can't remember anything. And my head hurts."

Her mother called out to someone in another room, and within minutes Beth found herself surrounded by unfamiliar visages.

It was hard to form impressions of them, with the buzzing in her mind. One young woman was blonde and very pretty, but her pettish pout made Beth want to sink away under the bedclothes.

Beside the girl stood an older man—my father? Beth wondered —who shifted from one foot to the other impatiently, as if he had been in the middle of something and were in a hurry to return to it.

To her dismay, Meridan had risen and stepped away, and now he left the room entirely. His expression had been transformed as he went, and the last look he cast her way was almost hostile.

I can't face these people now—I truly can't, Beth thought. Why don't they see how weak I am and go away?

But they continued to yammer at her with questions that she couldn't answer. Why had she ridden so fast? Whatever had got into her, running at the fence that way?

Finally, a maid entered the room and informed them that luncheon was served. At that, they departed with what seemed to her to be relief.

"Shall I bring some lunch, then?" asked the maid. "You've had a hard morning, from the looks of it, even if it did last only a few minutes."

Somehow, Beth was able to remember that maids oughtn't to speak so familiarly to their betters, although she wasn't sure how she knew that she herself wasn't a maid. But she was grateful for the woman's cheerfulness, so she merely gave her assent and lay back in relief.

The woman left. Alone, Beth tried to assemble her thoughts. She wasn't even quite sure that they *were* thoughts, or that she existed at all. What a strange experience this was! She must remember to tell . . . but she'd forgotten who it was she wanted to tell such a thing to.

The rest of the day and night passed in a haze, with brief periods of wakefulness alternating with deep sleep and a dazed semi-awareness. She knew at one point that the doctor had come, and that he was a wizened little man with a bald head, but she hadn't the faintest notion of what he'd said.

The tall man who was her most welcome visitor seemed purposely to avoid her when Beth was alert, but slipped in at other times and she would drift to consciousness to see his face over hers, watching.

Perhaps his concern derived only from his ownership of the mare that had thrown her. But even though she couldn't place him, Beth knew she hoped there was more between them than that.

The next day she found to her relief that at least she recalled the events of the previous day. It had seemed not at all unlikely that she might continue to exist in a memoryless state, but now she felt more certain that she could indeed retain things and might eventually recover the past, as his lordship had said.

The doctor came again, and she asked him.

"Absolutely," he nodded after a small application of leeches. "The bad blood is almost removed. It was the shock of the fall that disturbed . . . but I needn't bother a pretty young lady like you with such details. You'll get your memory back a bit at a time, Lady Elizabeth, though there may be some blank spots for quite a while.''

Lady Elizabeth. Her name was something to mull, after he was gone. She must be someone important, to be called lady.

That afternoon her mother came in to see her again. "We've stretched our welcome to the limit, although the marquis would never say so,'' she said disapprovingly. "There are plans for Hester's birthday ball that must be moved forward, and so we're to return tomorrow to Fairchild House.''

An image of a Tudor manor flashed through Beth's mind, and she sensed it must be Fairchild House itself, and that it must be her home.

But when his lordship returned later, he would not hear of Elizabeth's being removed.

"She is far too delicate,'' he insisted. "The doctor has left strict instructions that she must not leave her bed for several more days.''

"Impossible!'' cried Lady Fairchild. "It's not my wish to leave, of course, and Hester never says a word of complaint, but William is simply wild to be home. And you know, poor Hester will have her eighteenth birthday in little more than a week's time, and we must get on with the plans. You do plan to attend, I pray, my lord?''

"But of course." His lordship nodded in a civil manner, although Beth sensed from his stiffness that he disapproved of her mother's attitude. "In the meanwhile, you may leave your daughter here in the care of my housekeeper. May I suggest that you send some of her garments, and perhaps she will be well enough to travel by the time of the birthday ball. In that case, I shall bring her with me when I come.''

There were protestations and objections, but they were easily overridden—easily because her family did not really want to be plagued with her, Beth perceived with a stab of pain. She felt quite lost. Her memory might have provided her with some means of defending herself against their evident disregard, but now she felt stripped and vulnerable.

Later she heard the bustle of people moving about, and realised her family must be packing and departing. Quickly she reviewed what she knew of them. The blonde girl was Hester, and clearly not a special friend, for she'd only come to visit once. Her mother was lofty and appeared to resent having to bother with Beth, while her father also appeared annoyed at having to visit her.

There must be more of us than that, she thought dimly. Must be someone else or I'd never have survived all these years . . . .

When she woke again the house was quiet. The maid brought her tea shortly afterward, followed by a plump and cheerful woman who introduced herself as the housekeeper, Mrs. Wakeham.

"Well, 'tis a good thing you're not much bruised, although I'll warrant that head feels like a sack of cabbages," said the woman as she helped Beth change into a clean shift and washed her gently with a soft, damp cloth. "We wouldn't want his lordship to be seeing you looking like an old knocked-about turnip."

"I beg your pardon?" said Beth, more intrigued than offended by the woman's colourful speech. "I'm certain your master doesn't care much what I look like."

"Well, I'd not be knowing that," said Mrs. Wakeham. "But it would be a real shame, wouldn't it, you gone to all this trouble and then to look like a poor battered thing."

"Surely you don't think I did this on purpose?" Beth said.

Mrs. Wakeham clucked reassuringly. "I'm not saying I do. But as long as you're here . . . well, my lady, there's more than one way to saddle a horse, they say." And she bustled out of the room before Beth could close her mouth around words of protest.

Beth slept again, and awoke in early evening to find herself blinking up at her favourite pair of green eyes.

"My lord!" she said weakly, shaking her head to clear the dull edges of sleep away.

He drew back immediately, the tenderness in his eyes—or had she merely imagined it?—replaced by wariness. "Yes?" he inquired tonelessly.

"It seemed to me there was something I had just realised," she whispered. "Before my accident. It troubles me. I had meant to change something. Perhaps about myself. But now I do not know what it was."

"I'm afraid I can't be of much help there." Although his tone and expression had grown distant, he remained physically quite close, leaning over her in an almost protective manner. "I've no idea what you were about. Only that you insisted upon riding in the hunt, and borrowing my mare as your own was lame."

"How foolhardy of me," Beth murmured. "Did I do that sort of thing often?"

He nodded. "Racing in Hyde Park, damping your petticoats at balls. I beg your pardon. I should hardly have remarked on such a thing."

"It seems I had sufficient shortcomings to reform, then," she observed.

Beth, still feeling somewhat light-headed but otherwise a bit more alert than previously, raised herself into a sitting position. The marquis leaned forward to adjust her pillows, his arms reaching around her as he did so. A quiver of delight shot through her, but Beth knew instinctively that she must not reveal it or he would draw away.

She managed to keep still until he was finished, despite an intensely pleasant awareness of his tanned cheek only a few inches from her own. He finished his task and straightened, their eyes meeting for a moment before she carefully lowered hers.

"It is difficult for me to imagine what you say to be true, although I do not doubt your word," she resumed as if the interlude had never occurred. "It does not match my inclination at all. I think I would shudder to have all the world stare at me, and gossip about my behaviour."

"Then you are very much changed indeed," he said gravely.

Something tickled at the back of Beth's mind, some inconsistency in all this that hinted at an explanation, but she could not think of it. And who was this man to her, and why did he seem both drawn to and repelled by her?

"Do I gather correctly that you are my family's neighbour?" she inquired.

His lordship nodded. "Only some ten miles separate the two estates."

"I apologise for being so indiscreet as to injure myself on your property," she told him, and was pleased to see a smile tug at the corners of his mouth. "If I must behave shamelessly at times, I cannot see why I could not have restrained myself while on a visit. It is my hope that when I recover, I shall find some way to show my gratitude for your trouble."

A knock at the door was followed by Mrs. Wakeham, carrying a supper tray. His lordship—Brett, he had said his name was—rose quickly. "I fear it is I who have behaved improperly, in sitting alone with a young lady in her bedroom, but I had only meant to look in on you while you slept. Pray excuse me, Lady Elizabeth." Without waiting for a response, he strode out of the room.

Beth looked up plaintively as the tray was set on her lap. "Is he always so changeable, your master?" she asked. "One minute he seems quite pleased with me, and another as if I were a most unwelcome intruder."

"A good sign, very good indeed." Mrs. Wakeham adjusted the pillows further and sat down beside her while Beth ate. "A man's a bit like a hedgehog you know. Don't bother to raise its quills when there's no danger around."

"But I'm not dangerous," Beth said.

"You should be," reproved the housekeeper. "Do the man good. Don't know enough to keep from poking himself with his own quills, if you ask me. But then you didn't, did you?"

Beth ate quietly after that, but was able to arrive at no further conclusions.

In the days that followed, she gradually became able to walk a few steps, and to dress in the clothes her family had sent over.

Bits of her memory began to return. First she had an image of a kindly young woman whom she placed at last as her older sister Mary. Then she recalled their town house, and her come-out ball, and, to her chagrin, fragments of indiscreet behaviour on her own part, just as the marquis had described.

Her distress was intensified by the realisation that her host came less and less frequently to see her, and when he did, his manner was cold and bordered on the brusque.

The change in him puzzled her. No doubt her hoydenish activities in London had estranged him, but she was careful now to behave with utmost propriety. There must be something more, yet what it was, she could not guess.

It was on the fourth day that she first ventured out of the house, on a short walk to the stables, leaning on Mrs. Wakeham's arm. It was Beth's hope that by seeing the mare Fancy, she might bring back more of the accident itself, which was still a blank to her.

The smell of the animals reached her first, and there was something reassuring about it. Surely riding had indeed been a pleasure to her, and a means of escape. Escape from what? she wondered immediately. From her actions, it had sounded as though she must relish the limelight.

They entered the stables, their eyes momentarily blinded by the dimness. With the groom's guidance, Mrs. Wakeham escorted her to a stall in which stood a mare that started back nervously at their approach.

"She's a high-spirited one, isn't she?" Beth commented. "I suppose I must have felt quite sure of myself to have ridden her."

"Must have been something that frightened her," the housekeeper said. "She's no rabbit to take to the ground at the sight of a fox."

"Of course you're right," Beth agreed. If only she could recall what it was! She couldn't shake the feeling that the events of that day had been highly significant, and that somehow she must find a way to remember them.

They waited a moment longer, in case she had any revelations, but there were none, so they turned back toward the house.

As they emerged from the stables, she became aware of Lord Meridan's inscrutable gaze on her, and looked up inquiringly.

"Has anything come back to her?" he said, addressing Mrs. Wakeham.

"I fear not," said that woman. "You don't suppose this memory loss is permanent?"

He shook his head. "I find such a thing highly unlikely."

As they spoke, a small animal flashed around the corner of the stables and through the dark corners of Beth's mind. Even as she registered that it was only a tawny cat, she heard herself saying, "The fox! It was the fox!"

The marquis frowned. "The fox startled Fancy? But you were not close enough for that."

"No." Beth shook her head, not sure what she meant. "It was me. The fox was me."

She realised her two companions were exchanging a knowing glance over her head. They think I'm delirious, she realised as she was guided back to the house with soothing clucks from the housekeeper. But I'm not.

Lying in bed that evening, she reviewed her insight of the day, still unclear as to precisely what it signified. She had been the fox, of that she was sure. Someone had been pursuing her, hounds and horsemen. . . .

For one terrified instant, she wondered if there had been some evil game perpetrated upon her, and some conspiracy to hide it from her. Could they really have chased after her instead of a fox? Had her parents really wished to rid themselves of her that greatly?

Nonsense, she scolded herself. This was a civilised household, and a civilised country. Besides, she had truly seen a fox.

Giving up at last, she sank into a restless sleep full of pounding hoofbeats and aloof green eyes.

The day of her return home grew nearer. Beth dreaded arriving at that Tudor house, dreaded the look she would find on her mother's face. Why should she be so despised? Perhaps it had been her own manner of conducting herself, but surely a loving parent would forgive even that when a child had been severely injured.

Pronounced able to join his lordship for dinner, she allowed the maid to dress her in a rose-sprigged muslin gown. Despite its demurely high neckline, the thinness of the material revealed more of her figure than she would have liked, but it was the least revealing of any of her evening dresses.

Beth travelled shakily downstairs with only a minimum of help from Mrs. Wakeham, although she hadn't descended since the day she visited the stable. Lord Meridan, dressed severely in black coat, waistcoat, and trousers, took her arm at the foot of the steps and escorted her into the dining room.

"You are near recovered then?" he inquired. To her relief, he seated her at the place beside his own rather than at the foot of the long table.

"I suppose I must be," she told him, tasting the wine he poured for her. "But there are so many questions still unanswered in my mind."

"You are not still imagining yourself to be a fox, I hope?" He took his seat and signalled to the footman that the meal was to begin.

"I don't think I literally believed myself to have been a fox," Beth said. "It was only that I felt as if someone, or more likely a great many people, were chasing after me, intent on doing me harm."

He stared at her in surprise. "I should think it was you who put yourself in harm's way."

"Was I so very disgraceful?" she forced herself to ask, although the topic was painful to her. "Have I done any great harm, my lord?"

He stared into his wine glass with such intensity that she thought for a moment it might shatter. "I'm afraid you have," he replied. "But that cannot be helped now. Your task is to get well."

"What harm was that?" she begged, and was irritated when the servants began parading in with the simple dinner of roast chicken and venison, green beans, and small buttered potatoes. The interruption seemed to last for ages.

Finally they were alone again, and the marquis's face showed clearly that he had not forgotten her question. "I think that as you are beginning a new life, it would be best not to dredge up past mistakes," he responded at last, and although she tried several times more to pry the truth from him, he determinedly turned the conversation to her sister's upcoming birthday party.

With an inward sigh, Beth relinquished her desire to continue on the former subject and bowed to his wishes. "Hester is rather my mother's favourite, or so I formed the impression the other day," she told him.

"Your sister is a sweet and docile creature, as it appears, although I do not know her well." His words were approving but the tone indifferent, for which Beth found herself grateful.

They chatted of one thing and another for the rest of the dinner, and to her surprise Beth found herself quite comfortable in his presence. As long as the topic remained impersonal, he too seemed to relax, although he appeared somewhat surprised to find that her sympathies lay greatly with the poor working people in matters of enclosure and import restrictions.

Most of their talk was of a less political nature, however. She learned that her sister was to have her come-out in London that spring, and that she herself had been presented to society only the year before. Those facts stirred distressing twinges in her mind.

Hazily she recalled having seen the marquis in London, and wishing in vain for his good opinion. He was known to be a hard man with his enemies and a kind, generous one with his friends; that much she had no difficulty believing to be true.

Once the meal was finished, his lordship returned her to the care of Mrs. Wakeham and made his way toward his study. Watching his retreating back wistfully, Beth wished she knew what terrible thing she had done to alienate a man who was so dear to her.

Why, I'm in love with him! she realised as she mounted the stair, and hoped the shock on her face did not transmit itself to Mrs. Wakeham's notice. I love him, and some part of him cares for me, but I have driven him away. I have done something shameful, for which he cannot bring himself to forgive me. And I cannot even remember what it was!

She sat alone that evening by the window of her room, staring out across the placid landscape of Kent. More bits of memory danced through her brain—her own inability to please her mother, Hester's calculated perfection, the coolness with which she herself had been received into society.

It was near sorting itself out, Beth felt quite sure. Perhaps in the morning she would remember it all, and only just in time, for tomorrow she was to return home.

== 3 ==

"THE LACE IS quite low enough. I would not want to look like Beth," Hester sniffed, examining her image in the looking glass. Her dress was of white muslin, correctly modest for a young lady not yet out, but very finely made, with seed pearls worked across the puffed sleeves and high-waisted bodice and white ribbons woven through the hem.

"It does fit so very well, and I declare, she does look such an angel!" Lady Fairchild exclaimed, and the dressmaker nodded, pleased. It had been a rare honour for a village seamstress to be selected to make this dress, even though it was only to be seen at a country ball.

Hester shed the gown, her mind flying ahead to that evening. "The marquis is sure to attend, since we have had no word otherwise," she observed as she and her mother retreated to that lady's sitting room. "Unfortunately, he must bring Lizzie, mustn't he? But surely she's unwell. A ball would be far too rigourous for her."

Her mother shrugged. "With Beth's constitution, one cannot be sure. At times I think she's more of a horse than a girl."

Hester giggled. "Yes, I can see her taking the bit between her teeth. You're quite right, Mother." Her expression sobered. "Oh, dear. You don't suppose she'd embarrass me? Mother, we couldn't keep her away this season, do you suppose? Her injury might provide an excuse. It's only that I'm so afraid she'll disgrace me, and everyone will think of me as nothing but that hoyden's sister."

"Nonsense." Lady Fairchild poured tea into a paper-thin china cup. "Once the ton sets eyes on you, they'll forget Beth ever existed."

Hester sighed, but she knew better than to pursue this line of conversation. She had been seeking an excuse to prevent her sister from coming to town that spring and interfering with her own debut, but she feared to stress the point too strongly. Her mother was quite convinced of Hester's angelic nature, and that young woman didn't wish to correct the impression.

"However," Lady Fairchild continued, "I do assure you that if her behaviour becomes a scandal, I shall not hesitate to put her in her place. She will not be allowed to shame you."

Satisfied, Hester busied herself with examining the guest list. "Perhaps Sir Percy Stem might entertain Beth. He's something of a loose screw himself, I've heard, although they say he and Lord Meridan are friends."

"Oh, I don't know." Her mother stared thoughtfully out the window. "He's a lively sort and given to escapades, but comes of a respectable family. Unfortunately, his father gambled away most of the money. But yes, perhaps he would do for Beth."

"Now who is this?" Hester frowned at an unfamiliar name that had been added to the bottom of the list in her mother's handwriting. "The Viscount Winston? Who is he?"

"A houseguest of Mr. and Mrs. Tonquin," said Lady Fairchild. "No doubt someone they have in mind for Alicia."

"Oh, how lovely." Hester smiled maliciously, then added quickly, "I mean, how lovely for her if she were to become engaged so quickly. I'm sure if her parents have invited the viscount to visit, he must be quite important, even if we have never heard of him."

Privately, she hoped the viscount was elderly and balding with a wart on his nose. It would serve Alicia Tonquin right.

The girl was of the untitled nobility, and certainly respectable, but she had no right to attract the attention that she did. Men seemed to admire her raven hair and flashing black eyes excessively, although Hester had always privately thought that there must be gypsy blood in the family.

Alicia had never shown the proper deference to her betters, and had done her best to be sure everyone in Lenham heard of each of Beth's exploits. As a result, Hester had been forced to suffer considerable embarrassment.

Now Alicia was to have her come-out the same season as Hester, and, as her family was as wealthy as the Fairchilds, she bid likely to be Hester's chief rival for the attention of the young bucks in London. No doubt she would continue to make sure everyone knew whose sister Hester was.

The sound of carriage wheels outside drew Hester to the window. "Our guests are starting to arrive!" she cried. "Mother, whose carriage is that?"

"Lady Smythe, I believe."

Soon a barouche followed the larger vehicle into the drive, and then a cabriolet. For the next few hours, Hester had little to think about besides making their guests at home and hoping that somehow Lizzie would be delayed.

"I have remembered several things more," Beth told the marquis as they rode together in his phaeton across the familiar landscape of orchards now redolent with apple blossoms. "My visit with Fancy was more productive than I at first suspected."

He merely clucked to the horses and stared straight ahead. Beth hesitated, glancing at his stern profile and yearning to reach out and touch his cheek. If only she knew what she had done to make him her enemy; if only she could turn back the clock and undo the harm.

The silence lengthened, and she resumed her one-sided conversation. "You know how absurd it sounded when I said that I was the fox?"

He nodded and looked at her for a moment, but still said nothing.

"I was trying to save the fox."

He digested this for a moment before replying in a choked voice. "Save the fox?"

"While we were riding, I saw it dashing ahead of the hounds, and suddenly I realised that I was exactly like it," Beth said. "I was a fox of a sort, and there were hounds pursuing me—not real hounds, of course. Does this make any sense?"

"None at all."

"No, of course not." She stared down at her hands. She

couldn't tell him that she had ridden in the hunt in the first place because she was hoping to attract his attention. How very coarse and forward that seemed now! She had hoped to be able to explain that her former outrageous behaviour had all been an act, but her courage fled before his icy composure. "Perhaps I'm still a bit weak in the head. You're right, it makes no sense."

Tears stung at her eyes and she forced them back as he turned again to look at her. A strange vulnerability glinted in his face for a moment, as if he realised that she had been about to confide in him and had drawn back, and now wished he could hear what it was she had to say.

But her nerve was entirely gone. Not only did she find his lordship increasingly intimidating, especially since experiencing the revelation that she loved him hopelessly, but Beth wished devoutly that every stride of the matched bays were not carrying her closer and closer to her unwelcoming home.

Soon they turned into the long drive, and ahead she saw a clutter of carriages before the front door. Beth's head began to spin at the thought of having to greet all those people.

"I don't feel entirely well," she said. "Could you perhaps take me 'round to the servants' entrance? I think it would be best if I went upstairs unnoticed. I fear I might swoon if I have to stand exchanging pleasantries with all these people."

"Of course." He guided his team off onto a side drive, and reached out, taking her arm to steady her. "Can you hold out a few more minutes?"

She nodded dimly. At any other time she would have relished his gesture of concern, but just now she was barely able to remain sitting upright.

Several jolting minutes later, they arrived. The marquis tossed his reins to a stable boy and slid down, then came round to catch Beth by the waist and lower her to earth.

She swayed on landing and leaned against him for a moment, her cheek pressed against the superfine of his coat. He seemed in no hurry to spirit her away.

"Beth! That *is* you, my pet!" Mrs. Archbold, the housekeeper, bustled out the door.

"I fear the drive has done her ill," Lord Meridan said. "If you will lead the way, I will carry her to her chamber."

"Of course." The woman muttered worriedly as she turned, and Beth felt herself lifted effortlessly in Meridan's arms and crushed against his chest, aware of each muscular movement of his body as he strode up the back stairs.

Although Lady Fairchild had been too caught up in greeting her new arrivals to notice her middle daughter's approach, Hester had not. Indeed, she had been keeping a sharp eye out for the marquis for several hours.

Annoyed that her sister's welfare had apparently inspired him to drive to the back of the house, Hester excused herself to go investigate. Thus it was that she was treated to the sight of the most eligible man of her acquaintance carrying her sister in his arms, like some figure from Mrs. Radcliffe's novels.

Hester strolled up in his wake at a dignified pace, arriving at Lizzie's room to see the marquis lay the fragile figure gently on the bed as Mrs. Archbold fussed with pillows and coverlets.

"How very kind you are," Hester said from the doorway, and noted with relief that her sister seemed to be too weak even to sit up and regard her. "One rarely sees a gentleman these days with such exquisite courtesy, Lord Meridan, to have bourne with an injured guest for so long and then carry her personally up the stairs. I applaud your kind nature."

Curiously, her flowered speech appeared to make no impression on him, whereas in Hester's limited experience, it had been her discovery that gentlemen were delighted to encounter such a romantic figure as she.

Instead, his lordship stood gazing for a lingering moment at her sister's still form, as if reluctant to leave. It was only when Mrs. Archbold intervened and assured him that all Beth needed was rest, that he turned toward Hester and accompanied her downstairs.

"'And how is my sister?" she enquired as they walked. "We have all been devastated with worry for her."

"Curious," he murmured. "I should have thought in that case you would have been to visit her."

Immediately, Hester saw her error and hastened to rectify it.

"I'm not surprised you should think so," she assured him. "Indeed, I begged to be allowed to drive over on several occasions, but Mother wouldn't hear of it. She was greatly concerned about this little ball of ours tomorrow night."

"One would have thought she would be more concerned about an injured daughter," he remarked.

"Well, you know Lizzie," Hester said gaily. "She's always in and out of scrapes, and one doesn't think of them as serious."

His lordship said no more, and Hester was left to mull whether she had made a good impression. His indifferent air gave her no clew.

The marquis's arrival in the drawing room occasioned cheerful greetings from the other guests. Alicia Tonquin made a very pretty curtsey, and Hester was hard put to maintain her own sweet air.

She noted without much interest the studious-looking young man sitting beside Alicia. The Viscount Winston, she presumed. He had sallow skin and rather thin hair, and wore an expression that showed plainly his thoughts were elsewhere.

The conversation touched briefly on Beth's injury, but his lordship said only that she was fatigued from her journey, and soon more interesting topics were raised.

Beth slept until past suppertime. When she opened her eyes at last, it was to see the one face dearest to her in all the world: her sister Mary's.

They hugged each other amid tears and exclamations. Mary had only just arrived and learned of Beth's mishap, and had hurried upstairs to sit by her side.

"I'm sorry to take you away from the others," Beth told her.

"Not at all." Mary smiled ruefully. "I had rather not have come, you know, but Mother insisted. I've left Henry with the babies and he's not pleased to have me away these weeks. In fact, the only reason I'm glad to have come is that I can tend to you, for you can hardly think I look forward to dancing and playing cards."

Beth sighed. Mary, who was the prettiest of them all, with soft hair even fairer than Hester's and blue eyes that wore an expression of genuine goodness, had never cared a fig for the life in London. She who might have had everything—popularity, renown, and her mother's admiration—had preferred to marry quickly and retire into the countryside, and had professed herself happy ever since.

Mary rang for a supper tray, and sat by Beth as she ate. It was only afterward that she ventured to raise questions about the accident.

Feeling more than a little embarrassed, Beth told her everything, about her unrequited love for Lord Meridan and her foolish behaviour in society, and her madcap decision to ride in the hunt.

When she came to her description of the fox, and how her insight had led to her downfall, Mary pursed her mouth thoughtfully.

"And now what do you propose to do?" she said when Beth had finished.

"I hadn't really thought about it," Beth admitted. "I suppose first I must get well. Most of my memory has come back, but not the part I need most."

"And what is that?"

"Lord Meridan says that I have done some great harm, and I can see it is something that has lost me his regard forever. Yet I cannot for the life of me recall what it might be."

"Surely he is not so intolerant a man as to hold mere youthful high spirits against you," Mary agreed. "And I am sure had there been some scandal, it would have reached my ears."

"Perhaps at some time it will come back, and if it does not, I shall have to ask him," Beth resolved.

"But what of you? Are you to return to London this season? And if so, how shall you go on?"

Beth had to admit she had given the matter little thought. Now, as her sister departed reluctantly at last to go downstairs for politeness's sake, she was left with a mind full of concerns.

Perhaps she should stay here at Fairchild House all season, but for the life of her she could see no merit in that. It would take more courage and do more good to return to London and let everyone see how she had changed.

Moreover, as she was past her first season, she must concentrate on getting a husband, although the prospect daunted her. She loved Lord Meridan, but she could not have him. It was unlikely now that she would charm anyone of sufficient station to impress her mother, and besides, she was persuaded that nothing she could do would bring her to that lady's good graces.

The other choice was to find some solid but unromantic man of respectable means and shape herself into a good wife for him. Many other women had done so, and considered themselves well off, but Beth felt sure she could never adapt to such a life, even if the alternative were to remain forever unwed.

In fact, the thought of dissembling at all disturbed her deeply. Her conduct that past year had been a lie; a well-meant one, perhaps, but a lie all the same.

I cannot change society, but I can change myself, she thought. I shall be demure but honest, and simply make the best of whatever comes as a result.

Whatever came, she sensed, would be dire enough to punish her threefold for her misadventures of the previous season.

"Of course you shall go to the ball tonight!" Mary stared in astonishment at her younger sister. "You say you feel well enough, so whyever should you stay away?"

"Because it is Hester's ball and I . . . annoy her." That was the blunt truth, reflected Beth, who was determined to apply her new rules of conduct to even the most intimate family conversations.

"Why should you care if you do?" replied Mary spiritedly. "She shows no great concern for your welfare."

Beth, who was sitting at a small table in her sister's room, breathed a sigh as she realised that, unintentionally, she had told only part of the truth. This business of honesty was more complicated than she had anticipated.

"There is another reason as well," she confessed. "I can hardly bear to see Lord Meridan dancing and flirting with the other girls while I sit on the side."

"Perhaps he will flirt with you as well." Mary was examining two dresses, both quite fine, as she tried to decide what to wear that night. Anyone else with Mary's wealth and beauty would have had a gown especially made, but it was characteristic of her not to have given the matter much thought until now.

"Hester is so much prettier than I, and so much more gracious, at least to those who don't know her well." Beth replied. "And Alicia Tonquin will be there as well. Did you see her last night? I think her quite beautiful, although sadly enough she hasn't the personality to match."

Mary looked up from her gowns and placed her hands on her hips. "Elizabeth Fairchild, you are to stop this nonsense at once! I don't know why Mother has persuaded you that you are in any way inferior in looks to Hester or anyone else. It is only that you do not fit the current fashions, but you are quite lovely in your own way."

Honesty went down to yet a deeper level, as Beth answered softly, "And then I am a coward, Mary. How can I face all those people after the way I've conducted myself? I can scarce hold my head up."

"Regardless of what Lord Meridan thinks, you've done no great harm!" Mary retorted. "There've been no duels fought over you, have there?"

Beth shook her head. "Not that I remember."

"No one driven to drink or suicide, I trust?"

Again the negative shake.

"In other words, everyone has survived quite nicely. And so shall you. Believe me, Beth, when one lives in the country and sees what is truly important—one's husband and children, and the livelihood of those who depend on one, and fairness in all dealings—the activities of the beau monde in London come to seem trivial in the extreme."

Unfortunately, the opinion of Lord Meridan was anything but trivial to Beth, yet she knew she would never escape the night's entertainment. Acquiescing at last, she went to her room to see which of her gowns from last season would suit.

It was there that Lady Fairchild found her a short time later. Beth looked up to see her mother, frowning, in the doorway.

"Mother," Beth began. "Mary says I should attend tonight."

"I suppose we shall have to put up with you."

The words cut deeply, especially as this was only the second time Beth had seen her mother in a week, and there had not even been a hint of concern for her recovery.

"I could plead the headache, if you think it best," Beth offered.

Lady Fairchild ignored her words, walking over to examine the green silk gown Beth had been studying.

"The neckline is far too low," she chided. "Indeed, all of your dresses are made in this abominable manner. I should never have given you such a free hand."

Honesty, Beth found then, does not stop when it becomes inconvenient. She opened her mouth to issue some soothing reply, but instead out came the words, "It was not precisely that you wished to give me a free hand, Mother, so much as that you could not be troubled to come with me to the modiste."

"I beg your pardon?" Her mother stared at her in astonishment. "What did you say?"

"The truth," said Beth. "Had you cared more about me, you could have exercised a great deal more guidance last year and saved us both considerable heartache."

"Are you blaming me for your execrable conduct?" Lady Fairchild's eyes flashed dangerously at this sign of rebellion from her least favourite child.

"No." Beth wished she could sink through the floor. Whatever had possessed her to speak this way to her mother? "No. Let us return to the dress. I shall have Bertha stitch in some lace, if she is not too busy maiding our guests."

"That will have to do, I suppose." Lady Fairchild swung about and strode to the door, then turned back. "I will not countenance impertinence, Elizabeth."

"No, madam," her daughter said meekly.

She sank onto the bed in dismay as soon as her mother had departed. Now she was more afraid than ever of what would happen tonight and this season. Yet she could see no halfway point. She could not mince and smile falsely like Hester; nor would she return to her former method of attracting masculine attention. She would be herself, and disavow all falseness.

But what a pack of trouble that promised to be!

=4=

TO HER DISMAY, Beth found that her memory had not recovered as much as she thought. Joining her parents and sisters outside the second-floor ballroom to welcome their guests, she discovered that of those who greeted her knowingly, many looked not at all familiar.

Despite Beth's attempts to signal Mary, she was unable to convey to her family that she needed their assistance. As a result, she was forced to pretend acquaintance with people who, at the moment, were total strangers.

One florid woman, who wore a mauve turban aflutter with ostrich feathers, clucked and fussed over Beth for several minutes, much to her embarrassment.

"And you must promise to call upon me as soon as you arrive in London," the lady insisted.

"Indeed, I should be glad to do so but I fear the fall has damaged my memory and I cannot recall who you are," Beth confessed.

An expression of shock elongated the lady's face and sent the feathers bobbing wildly, like a pheasant in hunting season. "You cannot—why, my dear . . ."

"Elizabeth is jesting, of course," Lady Fairchild interjected with a warning frown at her daughter. "Naturally she cannot have forgotten *you*, Lady Smythe." She turned to Beth for confirmation.

Dutifully, Beth opened her mouth to concur, but found herself saying instead, "I regret that it is so, Lady Smythe, but my recall has been much damaged. I did not know who you were, but now that my memory has been refreshed, I shall be delighted to make your acquaintance.''

Far from appearing mollified, Lady Smythe gasped audibly and moved away without a backward glance.

Other guests were waiting to pay their respects, so Lady Fairchild had time for no more than a furious glare, but Beth knew she had stumbled into her mother's ill graces once again.

Alicia, her dark beauty heightened by a pale pink gown, swept by Beth with only the most casual of greetings. She made it quite clear that she considered her hostess no rival at all for the coming season. And of course she was right, Beth reflected glumly.

Behind Alicia came her father, Mr. Tonquin, and a shy young man.

''Are you acquainted with the Viscount Winston, Lady Elizabeth?'' inquired Mr. Tonquin, a short, roundfaced gentleman, as he presented his companion.

''I'm afraid I don't know,'' Beth answered. ''I lost my memory in my fall during the foxhunt, and I can hardly tell my neighbours from total strangers. It is only by chance that I remember you, Mr. Tonquin.''

He appeared taken aback at her candour, but the Viscount Winston showed his first sign of animation.

''You must tell me about this most extraordinary accident,'' he said, bending over her hand. ''I have a particular interest in matters of a medical nature.''

''Come along, John.'' Alicia Tonquin had returned, and Beth was surprised to note her pique at espying the family friend in conversation with another girl. ''We are holding up the line.''

''My apologies.'' He followed in her wake along with Mr. Tonquin, but favoured Beth with one last wistful glance.

She had no time to reflect on this state of affairs, however, for Lord Meridan was approaching.

''You appear recovered from your weakness of yesterday,'' he observed, giving her a stiffly formal bow. ''I trust you will soon find your accident naught but a faint memory.''

''Among other things,'' Beth murmured. About to pass by her, the marquis turned back with a quizzical expression. "I have just now insulted Lady Smythe by failing to know her."

"You might have pretended," he said with a puzzled air.

"Oh, no, not any more," she replied, but the crush of people accumulating behind him forced an end to the conversation.

The ballroom had been decorated in a pastoral theme, with potted climbing roses entwined about trellises and elaborate greenery distributed in clumps throughout the room. Beth was delighted to take advantage of one of these and sink onto a bench out of sight, where she could observe without being disturbed.

Although many of the guests were neighbours who had known the Fairchild family all their lives, there were also houseguests from London. Clearly Lady Fairchild thought it would suit her purpose to let a handful of acquaintances spread word of Hester's beauty and modesty, so that her success might be assured even before her come-out.

However, word of Alicia's charms was also likely to spread abroad, thought Beth as she watched the gentlemen flock to both of the younger girls.

She herself had been well attended at her come-out, but there had been a certain indifference on the part of the gentlemen that was not in evidence here. No one could dispute the gleams of ardour in youthful eyes as they gazed upon the contrasting countenances of Hester and Alicia.

With relief, Beth observed that the marquis was in neither group of admirers. Instead, he was speaking in a serious manner to one of the squires, most likely about some business involving poachers or broken fences.

The small orchestra began labouring at a quadrille, and soon the ballroom flowered with whirling ladies and gentlemen. Hester, although her dance card was no doubt almost filled by now, glanced frequently at the tall figure of Lord Meridan, Beth observed.

With curiosity, she noted that the Viscount Winston was dancing rather diffidently with Alicia. That girl responded to him with a continuing stream of chatter and flirtation, although Beth could not imagine that any of it was sincerely meant. The young man was too retiring and plain to draw Alicia's fancy. He must be wealthy, she decided; but the Tonquins were hardly on short rations themselves.

At the first interval, the viscount disentangled himself from Alicia and began circling the dance floor as if seeking someone. His eyes rested for a moment on Hester's vivacious face, but he won no encouragement there and soon continued his circuit.

Mary had been taken in tow by an elderly dowager who apparently wished to offer her unsolicited opinions upon modern methods of raising children. Her voice was audible from time to time, issuing forth such phrases as "in my day" and "havey-cavey business" and "young ragamuffins."

Children. Beth experienced a flash of pain as she thought of her young nieces and nephews. Would she ever have a husband and youngsters of her own?

"Lady Elizabeth." Lord Winston's voice startled her, coming so close by her elbow.

She turned sharply in her seat. "Oh! I didn't hear you approach."

"I trust I am not unwelcome?" The all-too-apparent timidity visible in his somewhat cloudy eyes filled her with compassion.

"No, indeed not, my lord," she responded. "Pray do join me."

"Will you not take a glass of ratafia?" he inquired politely.

"Thank you, sir, but I despise the stuff," she said. "Oh, do excuse my bluntness. It is a habit that has come upon me since my accident."

"You must tell me more about this." The chores of courtesy dispensed with, the young man perched eagerly beside her. "If you do not mind, will you describe to me exactly what proceeded, and of what your injuries consisted? It would be of the greatest interest to me."

Such an inquiry bordered on the improper, but Beth appreciated his directness. The viscount was clearly a fellow ill at ease in society but possessed of a fascination with medicine, and she admired his willingness not to bow to the pressures to keep his true self hidden.

So it was that she described the horse's run, without giving the background to it—a topic that did not appear to arouse his curiosity—as well as her mishap. She told how she had awakened in a state of ignorance, and the course by which her memory had returned in fits and starts.

"Tell me what medications and poultices were given you, and what the doctor said," he urged.

She did so, despite the indelicacy of the subject. The viscount quizzed her closely, oblivious to the music that had started up again. From the corner of her eye, Beth could see Alicia staring angrily about the room, but the potted shrubbery successfully kept the two from her sight.

"What do you think of my treatment?" Beth teased at last. "Does it meet with your approval?"

"Indeed, it seems the standard approach," her companion said earnestly. "Although I would not hold with bleeding under the circumstances. It is useful in treating fevers, but in an injury, I doubt that bad blood would be involved."

"It is my opinion that I should have recovered quite as well without a doctor as with one," said Beth, who had not given the matter much thought until that moment but found herself fully persuaded of the truth of her statement. "I do not believe doctors know much at all of the causes or cures of diseases."

The viscount nodded thoughtfully. "Have you heard of the work of Lady Montague, or Dr. Jenner?"

"Certainly." The crowd in the room had raised the temperature considerably, and Beth fanned herself to dispel the heat. "Lady Montague was much ridiculed for her belief that smallpox could be prevented, even though she saw inoculations in Turkey almost a century ago, is that not true?"

"Yet some of those whom she had inoculated here developed the disease as a result of it," Lord Winston pointed out. "What do you make of that?"

"Clearly, it was because they were given a small dose of the smallpox itself, whereas now Dr. Jenner has found that the cowpox will serve as well . . ."

"What indelicacy is this?" Lady Fairchild burst through their verdant screen, her voice pitched loudly enough for half the room to hear. "Do my ears deceive me or were you actually discussing diseases, and their treatments?"

As the orchestra had finished a Scottish reel, Beth supposed almost all the guests to have heard this tirade, and realized she was flushing a bright crimson.

"It is entirely my fault, Lady Fairchild," the viscount apologised. "I have taken advantage of your daughter's weakened state to encourage her to describe her injuries to me, as I take a particular interest . . ."

"Describe her injuries?" Once again, Lady Fairchild's voice rose almost to a shriek, and Beth began to wonder if it were not in fact her intention to humiliate her daughter. It would suit her as well as Hester to have the family disgrace remain in Kent that spring, she realised.

"Mother, pray calm yourself." Hester approached, her face a study in embarrassment.

"So! There you are!" Alicia had followed right behind. "Lord Winston, have you forgotten you extracted my promise for the next dance?"

"Oh. Well, yes I had," he admitted, much abashed. Rising, he took Beth's hand and peered imploringly into her eyes. "Please forgive me, Lady Elizabeth. It appears I have brought you much trouble, when I meant nothing of the sort."

"It is not you who have brought me trouble," Beth answered. She felt rather as if she were back on a runaway horse, but this time it was her tongue that refused to stop. "It is my own mother who shames me, by trumpeting the private contents of our discussion across half the room. Thus may a minor indiscretion be blown up into a scandal, albeit a rather silly one."

Lady Fairchild stepped back as though she had been struck. "I cannot have heard you correctly," she said.

"You will receive no apology from me, madam." However, Beth lowered her voice, grateful as Alicia tugged the viscount away and she heard the hum of conversation returning to normal among their guests. "However, if it is your intent to embarrass me into remaining at Fairchild House this season, I do not intend to submit like a naughty child."

"You will go to your room at once," snapped her mother, while Hester simpered in the background. "You are not too old to be beaten."

"Father would never consent to such a thing, and if you are looking for a scandal, madam, I assure you one will quickly follow if I am beaten in my present injured state," Beth retorted, standing up to face her mother. "I suggest you return to your guests."

For a moment, she watched disbelief war with fury in her mother's eyes. Then Hester intervened.

"Mother, with her headstrong nature, she could wreck our ball and my come-out as well," the younger girl said. "It is not necessary to complete this discussion here and now, is it?"

"You are right, of course," Lady Fairchild said. "We will take up this matter tomorrow evening when our guests have departed, Elizabeth." She swept away, but Hester lingered behind.

"You shall regret this," she hissed, her pretty face contorted with fury. "Just because you weren't the toast of London, you want to deny me the opportunity, don't you?"

"Not at all." The confrontation with her mother had left Beth feeling shaky. "Believe me, Hester, that is not my intention. I only want fair treatment for myself. See that I am treated as your older sister should be, and I assure you I shall do my best not to disturb your season."

Hester chewed on her lip indecisively. "You will not race horses in Hyde Park?"

"Oh, no." Beth shook her head.

"Nor wear your dresses cut so low you might be mistaken for a Cyprian?"

"Never again," she promised.

"How do I know this is true?"

"Because to the best of my ability, I shall never do or speak anything but the truth again," Beth said.

Hester eyed her uncertainly, but nodded at last. "Very well. Behave as you should, and I shall attempt to dissuade Mother from punishing you."

As the younger girl walked away, Beth found herself pleased by this unexpected truce. Perhaps the lifelong competition between them had distorted her view of Hester. Certainly it had all but destroyed any sisterly feeling between them. But once Hester saw that her sister truly wished her no ill, perhaps some semblance of friendship could be reached.

Before she could contemplate further, the marquis approached and bowed politely. "For someone so ill and helpless, you have not done badly tonight," he said sardonically.

"I hardly take pride in antagonising my own mother," Beth answered, more sharply than she had intended. Much as she admired Lord Meridan, she despaired of ever winning his good will, and she saw no reason to accept set-downs from him.

"That was not what I meant." His tone softened as his deep green eyes rested on her face. "You have stolen the heir to a dukedom from under the nose of one of the county's reigning beauties."

It took her a moment to comprehend. "The Viscount Winston?" she gasped.

"You didn't know?" He raised one eyebrow. "You surprise me, Lady Elizabeth. Anyone so adroit at handling her admirers could scarcely be so ignorant. But I must confess, it had appeared to me that your sister was unaware of young Winston's position, for she has been quite cool toward him."

Beth shook her head. "If I'd known that, I doubt if I'd have had the courage to speak to him."

"Do not try to bam me." Disconcertingly, the marquis placed her hand on his arm as he spoke. "It has been my impression that boldness is your predominant trait."

"I don't wish to argue with you." She tried to hold back as he pulled her toward the dance floor. "Whatever are you doing? I am much too weak . . ."

"Nonsense." As he swept her into his arms, she realised that the orchestra had begun a waltz. Hester and Alicia and the other girls too young to have been presented to society were obliged to stand on the sidelines, for they would have risked censure by publicly allowing themselves to be held in so familiar a manner.

But Beth was not so constrained, as Lord Meridan well knew, for she had won the permission of the patronesses to waltz at Almack's the previous year. Now he held her even closer than custom required, one hand firmly gripping her waist and his head bent so that one cheek grazed hers.

Over his shoulder, Beth glimpsed resentment blazing from Hester's eyes. The truce had been short-lived.

But she forgot her sister as the music caught them and she fell under a romantic spell that misted away all her resolutions. Despite his professed disdain of her, the marquis clasped her tenderly, and once his mouth grazed the side of her head with a gentle kiss.

Beth let the moment take her. Soon he would return to his former coldness, and soon Lady Fairchild would find some method of punishing her daughter—with Hester's encouragement—but for now Beth wanted only for this moment to last forever.

The heat and the nearness of the marquis combined to set her head spinning, and she swayed. Instantly, her partner changed their course and, without missing a step, waltzed her out through the open doors onto the balcony.

There they continued to dance until the music ebbed away. Afterward, Beth remained standing against him for one enchanted moment, her eyes closed.

His hand glided up her arm, tingling across her bare neck and tipping her chin upwards toward him. Before she realized what was happening, his mouth had closed over hers.

The demanding passion of his kiss called forth a longing of her own. Surely she should pull away, cry out, even slap him. But Beth could only do what she honestly wanted to, and that was to twine her arms about his neck and kiss him back with all her heart.

It was only as the strains of another quadrille floated out to them that Lord Meridan raised his head and stood gazing at her. Beth found her breath coming quickly.

"Yes, you are irresistible," his lordship murmured, but his tone was chill. "How artfully you seduce a man, Lady Elizabeth. You are well practised."

Stunned by his words, she stepped back and stared up at him in hurt dismay. "I have never . . ." she began, and then realised he would not credit the truth, that she had never before allowed a man to hold her in this manner.

Perhaps he was misled by her reputation, but that was no excuse for treating her in such a manner in her own home. "Clearly you are determined to despise me, no matter what I do or say," she finished.

His face remained impassive. "I have good reason to do so," he said.

"Then please explain it to me. You have hinted at some dark dealings in my past; since this involves me, surely I have the right to know of it." she answered.

"You know of it quite well." Anger edged his voice. "Do not play coy with me, my lady."

"You know full well that my memory is imperfect!" she retorted. "If ever I knew of what you speak, I no longer do. Once again, I ask that you explain yourself."

"How very convenient." His mouth tightened in sarcasm. "You forget Lady Smythe, who no doubt bores you, but not Alicia, who is a rival. You remember how to waltz and how to kiss, but forget that which is to your disfavour. I am not such a fool as some men."

"I do not expect kindness from you, Lord Meridan, but I did expect fairness." With difficulty, Beth forced back the tears that threatened to choke off her speech. "You appear to take pleasure in taunting me. Very well. I leave you to your sport."

She strode back through the doors into the ballroom. But she quickly found she had escaped from the frying pan into the fire.

Hester stepped from behind a trellis, eyes blazing. "You cheat!" she whispered furiously. "You thought I would not find out that Lord Winston is the heir to a dukedom! And then you had the temerity to waltz with Lord Meridan before everyone, when you know I had set my cap for him."

"I didn't know, Hester—" Beth began, but her sister wouldn't let her finish.

"The roses may have hidden you from everyone else, but I saw how you let him kiss you! Mother shall hear of this, rest assured, and she shall never let you come to London then!"

Hester stalked away without waiting for a response, and indeed, Beth had none to give. In fact, she began to think she would be happiest if she did not go to London after all.

Mary caught her arm as Beth swayed. "Oh, do forgive me, I've sorely neglected you!" cried her older sister. "You are pale as a ghost. You've overtired yourself, Beth!"

"Yes, I am tired," Beth admitted, allowing Mary to escort her from the room. "I'm tired of all of them, Mary. I'm tired of doing everything wrong, and having to fight everyone."

"Then you shall come and stay with Henry and me, and forget all about the ton," murmured her sister.

Beth nodded her agreement. But she was forced to admit, as she sank into her bed, that she would never forget the way the marquis had kissed her that night.

=5=

HESTER WAS HAVING a difficult time of it. She had managed to fall off her horse twice in the past hour, without incurring anything more than a few annoying scratches, and the Viscount Winston had taken scarcely any notice.

In fact, she had had little luck with him in the two days since she had arrived for Lady Smythe's house party in Buckinghamshire. Her only consolation was that Beth had been banished to Mary's house, although even that was uncomfortably close, just outside Amersham.

The viscount had not wished to discuss remedies for the headache or lotions for improving the complexion during their ride this afternoon either, and she was quite at a loss to think of any other suitable medical topics.

Instead, she had been forced to watch as Alicia continually teased and flirted with him, even now as their small band rode about the spring-fresh Chiltern Hills. However, he had taken scarcely any notice of Alicia either, appearing absorbed in peering nearsightedly at the thick beeches alongside the trail.

The only spark of interest he had shown all morning was when they passed the vine-covered brick cottage at Chalfont St. Giles in which Milton had lived while fleeing the London Plague in 1665. But Hester had never read *Paradise Regained*, which had been written there, or even *Paradise Lost*, and so had lost a chance at her own paradise.

"Perhaps if you could contrive to fall off the horse end-over-end you might attract his notice," suggested a masculine voice as a horse drew up at her side.

Hester turned in annoyance to meet the amused hazel eyes of Sir Percy Stem. "You imply that I have been deliberately unseated," she responded coldly.

The slender young gentleman, whose shock of brown hair kept falling into his eyes, merely chuckled. "My dear lady, you have done everything short of casting yourself into a duck pond to attract attention. Tell me, is this the latest social gambit? Why should you risk severe harm when you might better charm a man by giving him one of those delightful smiles of yours?"

Instead of smiling, she scowled. Sir Percy was a likable enough young gentleman, but his pockets were always to let, and furthermore, she had set her heart on marrying a title.

"I was not attempting to attract notice; I was attempting to injure myself," she retorted loftily.

His face registered astonishment. "Beg pardon?"

"Injure myself," she repeated. "Are you deaf, sir?"

She reined her mare about as the other riders turned back toward Lady Smythe's manor. A moment later, Sir Percy had ridden alongside again.

"Why the devil should you wish to injure yourself?" he asked in genuine puzzlement.

"Oh, you are the most exasperating a fellow!" Hester glared at him, then lowered her voice lest anyone else hear. "Because the viscount is fascinated by medicine, you looby. He spoke for simply hours with my sister Lizzie about *her* fall from a horse."

"Ah." He nodded knowingly. "And you wished to similarly entrance him." He shifted back thoughtfully in the saddle. "But might not this preoccupation with matters medicinal have unforeseen consequences?"

Hester sighed. "Such as what?"

"One can envision young ladies tossing themselves into the Thames to contract pneumonia, although, come to think of it, they can do that well enough by damping their petticoats as so many do," Sir Percy replied. "Or heavens, they might even tend the sick in almshouses so as to expose themselves to all manner of illnesses."

"You are making sport of me, Sir Percy!" snapped Hester, and once again urged her mare forward.

He bothered her no more that ride, and they arrived back at the manor to find a clutch of new arrivals.

Lady Smythe herself, resplendent in an outrageously unsuitable morning gown of gold velvet embroidered with scarlet butterflies, stood in the courtyard welcoming several men and women whom Hester did not recognise, as well as one whom she did—Lord Meridan.

She patted her somewhat wind-damaged curls. If Lord Winston insisted on remaining immune to her charms, at least she now had a clear field with the marquis. Thank heaven Lizzie, although only a few miles away, had been ordered by Lady Fairchild to give a wide berth to the house party.

"What a delightful way to usher in the new season," one lady was telling their hostess as Hester accepted a groom's aid and slid to the ground. "I do always enjoy a houseparty. It gives one the chance to see what everyone is wearing this year, and who is behaving scandalously with whom."

Hester planted herself in front of the marquis as he turned from instructing his coachman. He nearly ran straight into her.

"I beg your pardon, Lady Hester," he said, bowing over her hand. "I did not see you."

"Oh, it was entirely my fault, my lord, for I was not watching where I walked," Hester fluttered up at him. "I have only just alighted from a most tiring ride. I fear I lack my sister's stamina. But the countryside is indeed beautiful."

Lord Meridan scanned the other members of her riding party. "Ah, yes. The Viscount Winston. Undoubtedly an attraction that would lure any young lady into the saddle."

"Or out of it," interjected Sir Percy maddeningly, coming up behind her and shaking hands warmly with the marquis. "Good to see you again, Brett."

"And you, Percy." Lord Meridan slapped his friend on the shoulder. "Has it been a lively party, then?"

"Yes, indeed." He plunged ahead with aplomb. "Lady Hester has entertained us all today by casting herself about the countryside most painfully, although I fear she failed to suffer any wounds of sufficient medical complexity to intrigue anyone with an, er, medicinal bent."

"You are the most aggravating man!" Hester dropped her ladylike pose long enough to swat Sir Percy's arm with the handle of her riding crop. "You provoke me intentionally! Well, you shall not have the satisfaction of a response."

She stalked into the house, furiously aware that despite her words, she had given Sir Percy precisely the sort of response he wanted, and that he and the marquis were no doubt trading laughs at her expense that very moment.

Her temper was not improved by discovering that Alicia had entered ahead of her and was hanging onto the viscount's arm. In a pet, Hester stalked up to her room and stripped off her riding habit without even waiting for a maid.

She flung herself across the bed in frustration. If only her mother had come with her, but Lady Fairchild had gone ahead to London to open up the townhouse and entrusted her daughter's chaperonage to Lady Smythe.

Things were not working at all the way Hester had planned. She rolled over on her back and stared up at the pale blue ceiling as she reviewed the events of the last week.

He mother had been suitably furious to learn of Lizzie's misconduct. She had readily banished her middle daughter to Mary's house in lieu of attendance at Lady Smythe's, but Lizzie had not seemed to mind at all. In fact, she had seemed perfectly delighted.

Furthermore, Lord Fairchild, who usually ignored family matters, stepped in when his wife declared that Lizzie was not to have another season. How was he to get this baggage married off, he inquired, if she remained mouldering at Fairchild House? And so Lizzie was to come to town after all.

Then there was this party. Lady Smythe's Georgian manor had seemed the perfect setting for Hester to begin her conquest of society, but it was not working out that way at all.

Oh, there were admirers enough, but the only one who had mattered until the marquis's arrival was the viscount, and he ignored her. He likely would have ignored Alicia as well had he not owed a guest's obligation to the Tonquins, but he might nevertheless end up marrying her.

Imagine, Alicia a duchess! Hester moaned to herself. And I would have to curtsey to her, and call her Your Grace!

She ground her teeth in annoyance.

Now the marquis had come, but Sir Percy had made it clear that he intended to attach himself to his friend and to continue to plague Hester with his infernal teasing.

What if she were to end up like Lizzie, without a decent suitor to her name? Hester clutched at her pillow so tightly she all but ripped the fabric. It wasn't fair! She did everything just as she should, not running about wildly as Lizzie did. Well, she would be admired in London, where the company was wider and no doubt more appreciative than here in the country.

Still, Hester was hard put not to pout at dinner, when she found herself seated next to an elderly parson who prosed on and on about the evils of drink, and Mrs. Tonquin, who could say nothing that was not in praise of Alicia.

She retired early, as soon as she could do so without arousing comment, and lay awake for hours wondering what she had done wrong.

Her demure manner and discreet flirtations had always succeeded before. Why was her experience so different now?

The more Hester thought about it, the more she came to a most disagreeable conclusion. The sweet manner she had adopted was of little use against the more sophisticated wiles of the bold Alicia.

She had always shone before in contrast to the rough-and-tumble ways of her sister. Indeed, Lizzie had always been nearby, as long as Hester could remember, since only a year separated them in age.

With Lizzie blundering about, Hester appeared the soul of grace. Amid Lizzie's great faux pas, Hester's devices appeared the result of delicacy rather than artifice.

It had been a mistake to separate herself from her sister, Hester realized with a shock. Well, she would have to do something about that. And the sooner, the better.

By quizzing the maid the next morning, Hester learned that there were a number of sights in Amersham that would justify an expedition.

She proposed such a journey at breakfast, and received a mixture of responses. Some thought the venture would prove amusing; others complained that they had ridden themselves into soreness, but Lady Smythe countered that objection by offering to put her carriages at their disposal.

"Are there any objects medicinal to be found in Amersham?" inquired Sir Percy with feigned gravity.

Before she could give him a set-down, Hester noted that the viscount had focused his eyes upon her for the first time since she had arrived.

"Ah," she temporised. "Well, perhaps there may be. I do not know the whole of Amersham. There are murals of educational value, I believe, in a cottage near the market hall, of Julius Caesar and Hector of Troy."

"Two topics in which you take considerable interest, I believe?" said Lord Meridan, and she guessed he had been inspired to jocularity by his friend's manner.

"I am always interested in learning about new things," Hester responded primly. "And there are a number of inns where we may take lunch, and some sort of monument to a group of religious fanatics who werre burnt at the stake."

"It sounds well enough," Alicia murmured. "What do you think, John?"

Her familiar use of the viscount's Christian name made Hester groan inwardly, but she determinedly maintained a pleasant expression.

"I don't wish to be disagreeable, but I had far rather consult my books," responded Lord Winston, twiddling his thumbs nervously. "I have hardly attended to them at all in the past week, and I fear I spend far too much time frivolously."

"Then I shall remain here also," said Alicia firmly.

It was time to play her ace, Hester decided, taking a deep breath. "I thought perhaps while we were at Amersham we could stop by my sister Mary's house and see how my sister Elizabeth is recovering from her fall."

The viscount perked up at once. "Truly? I did not realise she was nearby. Then of course we must go."

"Naturally," growled Alicia.

Hester ventured a glance at the marquis and was surprised to see him frowning fixedly. Perhaps he was annoyed by the memory of Lizzie's behaviour at his foxhunt. It seemed that if Hester pleased one gentleman, she must anger another.

Lord Meridan spoke. "I was not aware that your sister was staying near here. Tell me, Lady Hester, why did she not come to the party with you?"

"Because she is still rather weak and preferred to remain with Mary," Hester answered.

"Well!" A snort came from the very perturbed Lady Smythe. "I like that! As if I abuse my guests! Did she not think she would find adequate treatment here?"

Hester sighed. She had thought herself the mistress of tact, but she was learning that making one's way in society was far different from cozying up to one's adoring mother.

"Not at all, my lady," she answered wearily. "She did not wish to impose, I'm sure."

At last the party was gathered and set out together with many grumblings. Having organised the event, Hester found herself responsible for its success, and so felt required to take the least desirable seat in a rattling old chaise next to a foppish young man and Mrs. Tonquin.

The visit to Amersham proved tedious. Hester quickly tired of gazing at gabled and timbered inns, thatched cottages, and cobbled courtyards. Moreover, she was sorely tried when they visited the murals to find Lord Meridan quizzing her closely about the histories of Julius Caesar and Hector, about which she knew next to nothing.

"You must understand, I wished to learn about them," she informed him at last. "Were I an expert already, I should see no point in coming."

"Of course," he replied smoothly.

Sir Percy moved to take her arm. "I feel my friend does you an injustice, Lady Hester. Why should a young woman of such beauty worry her head about the mistakes of people dead and buried two millenia?"

"Yes, why indeed?" sniffed Hester. "That is the sort of thing Lizzie might trouble herself about."

"Oh?" Lord Meridan, about to exit the cottage, turned in the doorway. "I was not of the impression that books and histories were of particular interest to her."

"Indeed they are," Hester said, happy to be able to converse with him despite the annoyance of Sir Percy hanging on her arm. "Before she went up to town last season, she spent most of her time reading and writing in her journal and other such boring things."

"But of course London changed her," said his lordship.

Hester shrugged. "She did her best to fit in, of course, but she was never very successful at it. If you ask my opinion, it did not suit her. She is a country mouse and a bluestocking at heart who would rather discuss Joan of Arc or the problems of orphans than know how to conduct herself in polite society."

"Most unfitting," murmured the marquis, leading the way outside so others could enter.

Hester warmed to her subject as she walked. Apparently even in her absence, Lizzie could prove useful. "Oh, indeed, she does concern herself with the most shocking things. The Luddites, for example, and the horrid way the weavers are smashing machinery. She used to prose on about that terribly."

"It is dull stuff," agreed Lord Meridan. "How could a woman of refinement and good character stoop to inform herself about the problems of the poor? It is scarcely her concern if the machines deprive them of their livelihood, or if by destroying the machines they in turn harm the factory owners."

"But why do we not go and see her?" chirped Hester, happy that she had held his lordship's attention for fully ten minutes. "I am sure she is not yet recovered enough to go racketing about the countryside and getting herself into scrapes again."

"Perhaps she will develop some interesting infirmity of a permanent nature," interjected Sir Percy. "That could serve two purposes. It could keep her docilely at home and assure her of the viscount's permanent interest. Indeed, marriage to an invalid would suit him admirably, wouldn't you say?"

"Oh, do be quiet," grumbled Hester, finally freeing her arm from his and stalking away.

They had lunch at the Swan Inn and then proceeded to the home of Mary and Henry St. Andrews, only a mile away.

"How lovely it's been these last few days." Beth leaned back on the blanket the servants had spread on the lawn, her needlework lying idle in her lap. "Mary, this does please me so much better than going to a party."

"It suits me as well," agreed her sister, playing with a toddler in the grass. "But you mustn't grow too complacent, Beth. You've not yet found yourself a husband. Once you do, you can retire to the countryside just as I have."

Beth closed her eyes and thought of the marquis, of his tanned skin beneath the thick sandy hair and of the green eyes that alternately warmed and chilled when he saw her.

"Perhaps I needn't marry," she said. "I could live here with you and Henry, and help take care of the children."

"Nonsense," Mary chided, tickling the little boy so he giggled. "You're behaving like a coward, Beth, and that isn't like you."

"Yes, indeed." Beth tossed her needlework into the air, catching it again in her lap. "I am pitching it all in, giving up, abandoning the field."

"All because you showed some high spirits last year?" Mary chided. "You are hardly the type to retreat . . . Good heavens, do you hear carriages? Who on earth can that be?"

"You can be sure of one thing," responded Beth, rising to carry her nephew into the house. "It isn't Hester come to fetch me to Lady Smythe's party."

But she was wrong, she discovered a few minutes later, when she descended the stairs to find herself facing everyone she had thought well out of her way—Hester, and Alicia, and Lord Meridan, and Lord Winston.

"Good heavens!" Beth said. "Hester, whatever are you doing here?"

"We've come to wish you well in your recovery," responded her sister.

Beth couldn't help but note the contrast between her plain cotton dress and the more elegant riding gowns worn by the ladies in the party. No doubt her sister intended to amuse her friends with the come-down of the naughty Lady Elizabeth.

She would not bow to such discreditable behaviour. Beth lifted her chin as she joined Mary in inviting the company in to tea.

"How sad that you must remain secluded," murmured Alicia as she nibbled on a cream cake in the parlour. "Such a lovely season it promises to be, too." She tossed back her dark hair in an eye-catching manner. "John and I will miss you very much."

So she had appropriated the viscount. Well, that was all right with Beth, but apparently not with him.

"Surely you don't intend to remain here all summer?" demanded Lord Winston, who had not uttered a word until that moment. "Has the doctor insisted upon it? There is one school of thought—not highly regarded, I admit—that one can actually become an invalid from being treated too much as one."

"I hardly think Lady Elizabeth is likely to become an invalid," murmured Lord Meridan drily.

Beth allowed herself one sidelong look at him, taking in his long, buckskin-clad legs as he sat on the sofa beside Sir Percy Stem.

Fortunately, Sir Percy did not share his comrade's dislike of her, she thought. He had been close friends also with Louis Chumley, one of Beth's suitors the previous year, and she had come to regard him almost as a brother. Unfortunately, her refusal of Mr. Chumley's proposal of marriage—he was far too impetuous and far too poor, and not at all the sort she could envision marrying—had also lost her Sir Percy's always entertaining company.

"Perhaps we could even prevail upon Lady Elizabeth to join us one evening," suggested Sir Percy with a wide-eyed look at Lady Smythe.

"Why, indeed!" she said. "She would be most welcome, if she can remember my name and abide my companionship."

Ruffled feathers, Beth saw. "I should be delighted to come, if I would not be intruding."

"You must come tomorrow night," Lady Smythe commanded. "We are having supper and a little dancing. Not a ball really, just a few musicians from the village."

To Beth's surprise, Hester beamed happily at her acceptance, although Alicia appeared predictably vexed as she tried in vain to interest the viscount in another cream cake.

"You do like small parties, don't you?" Alicia murmured at

last. "Of course, they would not give you scope for your activities, if you catch my meaning. But then, you would hardly dress or act in your London fashion here in the country, would you, Beth?"

It was almost a direct insult, and even Mrs. Tonquin looked displeased. "I'm sure my daughter didn't intend that the way it sounded," she smoothed.

"I'm quite sure she did, Mrs. Tonquin," Beth replied calmly, "although I appreciate your delicacy in the matter. I am fully aware that my scandalous behaviour offended many people, and raised sentiments of envy and resentment in many more."

Alicia gaped in astonishment as Beth continued, "But I cannot undo what is done. I can only show you by my conduct now that I have matured a great deal since last year. And I can only hope that the conduct of some others will be similarly ameliorated."

Lady Tonquin rose abruptly. "I find your manner toward my daughter insulting in the extreme."

"No insult was intended," Beth assured her, wishing once again that she could sink into the cellar. "I was only speaking the truth as best I could."

"There is much to be said for dissembling!" snapped the outraged mother, and stalked away without saying any of it.

As the others departed, the viscount paused to add how much he looked forward to the next night. Alicia pulled him quickly away.

The marquis was the last to depart. "You realise that you are well on your way to being considered an eccentric?" he said as he bowed politely over her hand.

Beth's eyes met his for one riveting moment, and then she shrugged. "Is it always so hard when one tells the truth?"

"Fair dealing is forever difficult," the marquis assured her. "I do applaud your good intentions, but I fear your reform comes too late."

"Too late for what?"

Instead of answering, he merely tipped his hat and turned away. Angrily, Beth grabbed his arm and whirled him around before he could realise what she was about. Mary gasped at her bold action but kept silent, and fortunately the others had all gone outside.

"Why you insist on playing this childish game. I cannot for the life of me understand!" Beth said. "I refuse to allow you to continually chastise and condemn me. Explain yourself or be so good as to hold your tongue!"

This time Mary did step forward. "Beth, have you lost all sense of propriety?"

"Indeed." The marquis drew his arm away frostily. "Good day, madam." He addressed himself to Mary, ignoring Beth as he turned and strode down the steps.

"Oh, dear, you have offended him," Mary moaned. "Beth, whatever possessed you to say such things?"

But Beth could only stare grimly after the man she loved. It was hard enough that others despised her, but to have him join them and not even to know why was almost more than she could bear.

Still, she must try to control her tongue, she scolded herself as she turned away.

There was tomorrow night to be got through, and then the whole season. But with any luck, it would be her last.

=6=

IT WAS TEN years since Mrs. Ariadne Singleton had come out, but a decade had not dimmed her reputation for beauty and style. At twenty-eight, wealthy, widowed, and independent, she did not lack for admirers.

One could not entirely prevent the inroads of time, the missing tooth at the back of one's mouth or the skin roughened by too much white paint. But with enough money and skill, one could overcome almost anything.

It was as a result of her carefully cultivated artfulness that Ariadne Singleton arrived last of everyone at Mrs. Smythe's house party, giving the gentlemen several days in which to weary of the charms of the other lady guests. Indeed, she made her entrance only at tea time on the day of the supper party.

Ariadne was sharply aware of the impression she made, swooping into the blue saloon in her ruby velvet pelisse over a white carriage dress trimmed with red ribbons. The bright colour had been selected to set off her chestnut hair, while opals dripped about her neck to call attention to the unusual aquamarine of her eyes.

Even Lord Meridan was impressed, and he had almost tired of her last year. As a result, she had studiously ignored him for almost six months now. Indifference was the one sure way to bring a man back to one's bed.

A quick glance around the room told Ariadne who her rivals were to be this season. Alicia Tonquin she spotted at once for a raven-haired beauty who might in time learn the seductive arts, but the girl did have the annoying habit of clinging, and it was evident within moments that the Viscount Winston was not at all enamoured.

Lady Hester Fairchild bore closer examination, and Ariadne indulged in it after carefully seating herself as far from the window as possible. Only a fool showed herself in daylight, especially so close to two fresh young creatures.

Hester had the looks to be an Incomparable, the thick, fair hair and innocent blue eyes. But she readily displayed herself to be a milk-and-water miss, simpering up at the gentlemen in a most witless manner. Had she her sister's spirit, there would have been no stopping her, but thank heaven she did not.

It did not escape Ariadne's notice that Elizabeth herself was nowhere in evidence. She had heard some talk of a riding accident on the marquis's estate, and immediately took this to have been carefully engineered so as to throw the two together. Well, that silly chit might try every trick in her book, and all in vain. Ariadne had taken care of that.

She scarcely spoke during tea, only murmuring that her ride had wearied her, and did not glance once at Lord Meridan. Let him come to her.

It was too bad John Winston was a mere stripling lad. He was heir to a dukedom, and had been gaping open-mouthed ever since Ariadne entered the room. Yes, he would be an easy conquest, but he was not who she wanted.

Ariadne excused herself early on pretext of exhaustion and retreated to her room. There she consulted with her maid, who had already quizzed the other servants and learned what the other women would be wearing that evening. One was certain to find disaster if one appeared in a gown similar to that of another lady, Ariadne knew; no matter how much better one looked in it, one's distinctiveness was blurred. Furthermore, there was always the possibility that the other lady would look even better.

Now she selected a gown with a golden bodice, low-cut to show the creamy tops of her breasts, with small puffed gold sleeves slashed with white silk. The overskirt was of gold as well, embroidered with acorns and seed pearls, and the underskirt all of white. A diamond necklace and tiara completed the ensemble.

Ariadne had only begun to apply her complexion creams when her maid hurried into the room from another of her gossipy expeditions. "Mrs. Singleton!" she gasped. "Another guest has arrived!"

While the maid paused for breath, Ariadne swung around, her eyes glistening furiously. It might be Lady Jersey, or perhaps Lady Cowper—someone even grander than Ariadne, come to steal her glory.

"Well?" she snapped impatiently. "And who may this person be?"

"Why, it's Beau Brummel himself!" the maid managed to stammer. "He had been invited, of course, but apparently he was not expected."

"The Beau never is," Ariadne said, turning back to her mirror with satisfaction.

She had no doubt she would shine at this dance, and what better audience could there be than the close friend of the Prince Regent and the arbiter of elegance? Brummel had set new standards for men's tailoring, insisting that clothing be well cut and made of fine material rather than the gaudy stuff of the previous generation. He eschewed powdered wigs, as well, and insisted above all on cleanliness. But the Beau was no Puritan. He was known for his outspoken nature, and to win his approval was to be guaranteed success.

It was odd, Ariadne reflected, as she allowed the maid to help her into her stays. She felt almost as if she were coming out this season, as if everything were new for her. Or perhaps it was that she knew deep within that this was her last chance to snare the Marquis of Meridan for a husband. Lose him again, and she would have to satisfy herself with some old buzzard—a wealthy and titled buzzard, of course.

But I shan't lose, she told her flirtatious reflection. Whatever it takes, I shall win this game.

As the St. Andrews carriage turned into the drive to Lady Smythe's, Beth was wishing fervently that she hadn't agreed to come.

She wasn't so much bothered by the fact that her gown was from last year as by its glaring incongruity with her new personality. Heaven knew what imp had ever led her to select this glittery gold fabric with its plunging neckline; it had been most incorrect for a girl in her first season.

The maid at Fairchild House had packed it by mistake, instead of the more demure green one Beth had selected. It would be impossible to have another gown made in only a day's time, and nothing else she had brought with her was remotely suitable.

"You look lovely," Mary assured her, as if reading her thoughts. "It does bring out the red in your hair, which is delightful, in spite of what Mother may think. Doesn't she look wonderful, dear?"

"Mmmph." Henry St. Andrews grunted his agreement. An angular, thoughtful man, he was little given to company or to idle chitchat. Beth knew how much attending this party had cost him, and she smiled warmly at her brother-in-law. He merely harrumphed again, but she was well-acquainted with his kindly nature and felt that at least she had two friends in the world.

"We need not stay late," she told Mary. "My condition is well known."

Her sister merely nodded. "We shall see. I doubt Hester will need my watchful eye, as she is generally circumspect, but she thinks herself far more worldly than she is. And I believe you are not so much disliked as you would have me believe."

"I am as much disliked as it as possible to be, and no more than I deserve," groaned Beth as they pulled up before the house.

There was no great crush of carriages such as one might find at a large ball, only a half-dozen vehicles that had brought some of the more esteemed neighbours. This was, as Lady Smythe had said, merely a supper dance.

The festivities were already under way, much to Beth's relief. The dancing was to be in a large parlour on the ground floor, and the musicians were tuning up their instruments. A number of ladies and gentlemen stood about sipping ratafia, orangeat, port, or sherry, chattering amid the flutter of painted hand-held fans.

Surrendering her pelisse to a servant, Beth looked about for her sister. She soon spotted Hester standing with Alicia, Lord Winston, and Sir Percy.

"Go on." Mary gave her a playful shove. "Greet your sister and force yourself to be pleasant. It will do you good."

Beth sighed as she crossed the floor, aware of a ripple of comment that trailed along behind her. It was the gown; they must be saying that here was that outrageous Fairchild chit again. Well, they would soon see that she had changed.

Once she would have waved gaily to everyone, and called out loudly to her sister. She had thought her cheery bluster created the illusion of being well-liked. Now she shrank from the memory. How they must have laughed behind her back!

Instead, she glided quietly to stand beside Hester, nodding politely to the company.

"What a splendid gown," murmured Alicia wickedly, being herself gowned demurely in pale blue. "How it does display your charms!"

"And considerable charms they are," put in Sir Percy. Beth shot him a grateful glance.

Hester pouted behind her ivory fan but quickly rose to the occasion. "Yes, dear Lizzie, how glad I am that you are well again," she said, and there was a note of sincerity to her voice that puzzled Beth.

"Have you any residual ringing?" inquired Lord Winston. At her puzzled look, he added, "in your ears."

"My ears have never rung, although many may have wished to wring my neck," Beth replied.

"And your memory?" the viscount pressed. "Has that all come back now?"

"Oh, yes," Beth said, and then remembered that the one thing she wanted most to know still eluded her. "Well, almost all of it. There are a few gaps yet, I suppose."

"You must tell me . . ." Lord Winston's words were cut off as Beth and everyone around her turned toward the doorway.

Entering the room was a couple stunning enough to take one's breath away, although in Beth's case the effect was more like that of having been punched in the midriff.

Lord Meridan's tall, well-muscled body was clad to perfection in a dark blue coat, a buff waistcoat, and dark blue breeches. Beside him stood Mrs. Ariadne Singleton, her hand resting on his arm in a light gesture that bespoke perfect confidence. She was taller than

Beth remembered, with an inborn dignity that almost persuaded one she must be of noble descent.

But what struck Beth most forcefully was the dress, gold and low-cut, so very similar to her own. What an awkward young imitation I must look! she thought, wishing she could dive into one of the potted palms.

How could this have happened? Ariadne bit her lip furiously. A dress almost exactly like her own, and on that outrageous young chit, Lady Elizabeth Fairchild!

To worsen matters, the gown showed her rival in her best light. Youth, of course, was on Elizabeth's side, with her fresh complexion and innocent brown eyes. The slender figure revealed by the dress was rounded enough to be feminine, without being in the least overdeveloped.

Ariadne felt like a trollop by comparison, with her large breasts and rouged cheeks. Quickly she steered Lord Meridan onto the dance area, but not before his eyes had taken in Lady Elizabeth.

"What an amazing coincidence," he murmured, his tone faintly mocking. "Two such different ladies with the same dressmaker."

"What a delightful melody!" declared Ariadne. "What tune is this, my lord? Do you know it?"

"It is called 'The Song of the Jealous Woman,' I think," he teased, dutifully escorting her into a set that had gathered on the floor to begin the dance.

Moving through the configurations, Ariadne felt the eyes of every man and woman in the room contrasting her appearance with that of the younger girl. Some of the men, of course, preferred her more voluptuous shape, but surely everyone else must be commenting on how very old Mrs. Singleton was becoming.

With fury, she noted the amused expression on the face of Beau Brummel. Slender, fastidiously neat, with short curly hair, the arbiter of fashion had not missed a moment of the two ladies' shock at seeing each other's attire.

Ariadne's displeasure deepened as she watched the Beau stride leisurely across the room and come to a halt by Elizabeth's side. He spoke, she nodded, and then he was leading her out.

The dance ended and a new one began. As one older couple had departed, there was space for another couple in Ariadne's set, and the Beau immediately seized upon it.

So it was that the two women, far from being allowed to separate themselves and maintain the fiction that the other had ceased to exist, were thrust shoulder to shoulder. It was with difficulty that Ariadne restrained the impulse to reach over and rend the girl's garment from bodice to hem.

Lord Meridan leaned close to Ariadne's ear. "Do try to disguise your revulsion, my dear," he said. "It is rather too plain for all to see."

Ariadne tried to force her mouth into a smile, but she felt as if her face would crack.

Thus far, Elizabeth had said not a word. Apparently the coincidence of the two gowns had abashed the girl, for last season she had been a chatterbox of the first order.

"And what do you think of Lady Elizabeth's gown?" inquired the Beau.

Ariadne glared over at him. "I think it most unsuitable for a chit of her years," she snapped. "It is a gown made for a woman of great sophistication, not some . . . some green girl barely out of the schoolroom!"

Elizabeth had turned pale. Surely she would respond in kind, and what a scene that would be. Ariadne knew word of it would spread all over London, but she had no doubt that she would come off the best.

"Lady Beth?" said the Beau. "May I ask your opinion of Mrs. Singleton's dress?"

"I agree that it suits her far better than me," the young woman said hesitantly.

"Perhaps." The Beau nodded. "But you have not answered my question. What is your opinion of it?"

"I think it far too gaudy, and cut much too low, and designed to attract the notice of every eligible gentleman in the room and some who are not so eligible," Elizabeth burst out. "I must have had windmills in my head the day I ordered it!"

She looked for a moment as if she would dash off, but her partner had caught hold of her arm and fortunately, at that moment the music began.

For once, Ariadne did not know how to respond. She was grateful for the demands of the dance as she tried to pull her thoughts together. Elizabeth's words had seemed more in chastisement of herself than of Ariadne, and yet they had been a clear set-down.

"I do not understand the baggage at all," she said aloud.

"She spoke quite clearly," said his lordship. "She does not like the dress."

"Then why is she wearing it?"

"Now, that is a mystery."

Beth herself was at that moment fervently wishing that she had never set eyes on the gold fabric, and wondering why she could not keep her mouth shut. Mrs. Singleton had always been cold to her; now she feared she had given the woman reason to take an active dislike.

"I apologise for my bluntness, sir," she told Beau Brummel. "I did not mean to make a scene."

"Not at all," he replied, handing her in a circle. "You merely spoke your mind, as I requested."

Beth looked up at him balefully. "You are a master at society's ways, sir. Perhaps you could help me understand something."

Her partner nodded, looking intrigued.

"I saw at once last year that I have not the looks nor the personality of the sort that lends itself to setting London on its ear," she said as they danced. "And so I embarked on a programme to establish myself another way, through boldness and daring."

He merely watched her with interest.

"But now I have had a change of heart," she continued earnestly. "I want nothing more than to be myself, to step aside and spend my time with the few people I care for. Yet there is one defect in my new character that seems certain to do me in, no matter how I try to control it."

"I do not think I can bear the suspense," he teased gently. "Pray tell me about this flaw."

"Honesty," sighed Beth. "Last season I was not honest at all, not in the deepest sense, for I was all pretense. This season I refuse to prevaricate on any subject. And what is the result? I insult people, I outrage my family, I disgrace myself."

The dance separated them then, and Beth had to wait nervously for his response. So preoccupied was she that she scarcely noticed upon whose hand she laid hers as she turned, until she found herself looking directly into the green eyes of the Marquis of Meridan.

"Oh!" she gasped, and watched amusement flicker across his face. "Oh, please tell Mrs. Singleton I did not mean her any ill. It is just this runaway tongue of mine."

"Let us hope it does not injure you as much as did a runaway horse," he observed, and passed her on to the next gentleman.

Beth returned at last to Beau Brummel, feeling flustered and a little faint. "I am not entirely well yet," she apologised.

"An accident such as yours should befall every lady in London," he told her as the dance swirled to an end. "I despise the petty arrow-shafts of words that are shot across the most polite drawing rooms, and which often do considerable harm."

"But honesty can be cruel as well," Elizabeth said.

"No one could possibly find you cruel." He guided her back toward her former companions. "Only charming and most refreshing."

He favoured her with a bow before turning away, leaving Beth staring after him open-mouthed.

"Whatever has transpired?" gasped Hester, catching her sister's arm. "I could not help overhearing his compliment to you. He has only to repeat it to his friends in town and your season will be made, Lizzie. Oh, how lucky you are!"

Beth had no time to savour this unexpected possibility, however, as the Viscount Winston was already at her elbow, requesting the next dance.

Alicia glared after them as they walked back toward the dance floor. "You can gild a lily, but it is only a common flower, after all," she snipped when they were out of earshot.

Stamping her foot in anger, Hester turned on her. "That is my sister you are speaking of!" she retorted. "Common flower, indeed! And who do you think you are, Alicia Tonquin?"

The other girl gasped and withdrew with a rapid flutter of the fan. Only then did Hester remember the discreetly annoying presence of Sir Percy Stem.

"Well spoke, Lady Hester, but more like your sister than yourself," he said. "Tell me, what prompted this uncharacteristic display of familial loyalty?"

"You do take every chance to provoke me!" she declared. "Surely even you can understand that whatever one may think about one's relations, one cannot tolerate such infamy from a girl of Alicia's stature."

"I see," he murmured. "If she were a countess, perhaps, or even a lady, she might abuse your sister to your face."

"Oh, you are hopeless!" Hester made as if to flounce away but found herself restrained by Sir Percy's hand on her arm. To her surprise, the sensation was not at all displeasing.

"I thought perhaps we might dance," he said.

"Oh, I am so sorry, but my card is all filled," she returned haughtily.

Sir Percy chuckled. "Nonsense. Do you think me such a green goose as to believe that? You have no card. This is only a supper dance."

Hester had quite forgotten that. Now she looked down at her hands in embarrassment, as if begging the fan to transform itself into a dance card.

"Come along." Firmly, Sir Percy grasped her arm and led her out onto the floor.

Dancing with him was not at all like whirling about with the other gentlemen who had partnered her before. He seemed not to be half afraid of her, as the others were, but quietly confident.

Yet at the same time he treated her with attention and care. His eyes did not rove around the room as some gentlemen's did; neither did he stare longingly into her face like some of the moonstruck striplings she had met.

Indeed, Hester felt quite comfortable, although irritated at the same time. After all, Sir Percy hadn't a feather to fly with, as everyone knew. He was no match for her.

Her feelings deepened to annoyance after the dance ended and Sir Percy stayed close by her, while Lizzie was selected for the next dance by none other than the Marquis of Meridan.

How very unfair it was! Hester reflected angrily. If only Mother were here! She would manage things, somehow.

At that moment, however, Beth was not feeling herself to be fortunate. While the marquis might look to anyone else like an admiring suitor, bowing over her hand, she was sharply aware of the cold glitter of his stare.

"So you have ingratiated yourself with the Beau," he told her in a low voice. "I congratulate you, Lady Elizabeth. Your scheme is working well."

"I beg your pardon?" She longed to slap his arrogant face. If only he didn't exert such a powerful spell over her!

"Despite my reputation as a Corinthian, I am sometimes painfully naive," he said as he guided her into an unwelcome waltz, the heat from his hand burning on her waist during the intimate movements. "Many things have become clear this evening."

"I have no doubt you will enlighten me," she retorted.

He nodded. "Your accident. It was staged for my benefit, was it not? Although perhaps it went farther than you expected."

"You flatter yourself," Beth snapped. "Do you truly think I would cast myself off a horse and risk life and limb to attract your notice?"

The marquis's face remained impassive. "Ladies have been known to do odder things. And you were well rewarded; almost a week alone with me at my home."

"Save for Mrs. Wakeham, the doctor, and my aching head," she answered. "You do demean yourself by thinking so low of me, my lord."

"Perhaps." Clearly he hadn't finished. "I would rather our conversation weren't overheard. Would you object to taking a stroll with me in the garden?"

"Oh, very well," Beth said ungraciously. She did not want his company just then, but he appeared bent on unburdening himself, and she supposed they might as well get on with it. What had provoked this sudden outpouring of suspicions? she wondered.

The March air felt refreshingly cool. Her hand placed lightly on the marquis's arm, Beth couldn't help reflecting how overjoyed she would be to walk with him like this, were it under other circumstances. But it was not, nor would it ever be.

"This newfound honesty of yours," he went on. "A very clever ruse, after your stratagems of last season did not work out as you planned. Now you have managed even to impress the Beau, and who knows to what heights you may rise?''

''Or to what depths you may sink?'' she murmured.

''You do not care for the truth, at least not when I am the one speaking it,'' he said coldly.

Beth pulled her hand away and faced him. ''This is not truth at all, but how am I to refute it? A lady's reputation is a fragile thing, my lord. I have no witnesses to my heart. Very well, here is the whole truth. I rode in the hunt to attract your notice.''

She went on, ignoring his look of surprise. ''In truth, I was riding toward the head of the pack, thinking that somehow I might speak with you, or otherwise draw your attention. But I did not plan to fall upon my head, I assure you. My esteem for you does not extend quite that far. As for my reform, it is indeed real. I had no idea it would impress anyone; in fact, it has mostly brought me trouble.''

His eyes searched hers. Unexpectedly, she sensed a yearning in him to believe her, but it passed almost as soon as it had come.

''I might credit what you say, were I not acquainted with the matter of Louis Chumley,'' said his lordship.

''Louis Chumley?'' she repeated. She remembered the man, barely more than a lad of some twenty or one-and-twenty years. He had lurked among her crowd of suitors the previous season, more drawn by her family's wealth than by her own charms. After her father rejected his offer of marriage, she had not seen him again.

''Do you deny the acquaintance?''

''Not at all,'' she said in confusion. ''He asked for my hand and my father refused him. He thought him a fortune hunter, and indeed, my affections were not engaged. Nor were his, I think.''

''There you are wrong.'' The marquis stared off into the garden, at the pattern of moonlight filtering through the benches. ''He told quite a different story.''

She waited quietly until he continued. ''Louis adored you,'' the marquis went on at last. ''He said that you flirted with him, gave him hope, and then laughed at his aspirations. In despair, he set off for America to seek his fortune.''

Confused, Beth watched a deep sadness settle across his lordship's handsome features. ''But I can scarce remember him,'' she protested. "Surely I would not intentionally have behaved so . . ."

Her voice trailed off and he turned to her questioningly.

"I'm afraid I can't say for sure," she admitted finally in a small voice. "There are still matters that evade my memory. Perhaps this is one of them, and yet I cannot believe it. But surely, my lord, it cannot be so terrible that a young man's heart should be broken? It is a common occurrence. Even that he set off for America, in his impecunious position, was not unwise."

"But most unfortunate," he said gravely. "His ship was sunk in a storm a week out to sea, and all on board were drowned."

Beth stood silent. The moonlight had turned to tendrils of ice, and the music behind them shrieked of a devil's dance. She had been responsible for a man's death.

"That is all I have to say," commented the marquis at last. "Shall we go in?"

Beth nodded numbly, and allowed him to lead her inside. As soon as she found Mary, she plead a sick headache, and was whisked away by her worried sister and relieved brother-in-law.

As she was going out the door, Beth caught a puzzling glimpse of Ariadne Singleton. She could almost have sworn the woman wore an expression of triumph.

=7=

NEITHER SIR PERCY nor Lord Meridan could keep his mind focussed on a hand of whist, and so both retreated after minor losses to their favourite corner at White's.

From where they lounged, they could see the bow window overlooking Bond Street that had become the exclusive preserve of Beau Brummel and his friends. One could, if one wished, learn who was anyone in London by watching to see whom the Beau greeted and whom he snubbed.

However, neither man was much interested in such foolishness, both having deeper matters on their minds.

Brett Meridan, staring down at his highly polished Hessian boots, was wondering why in heaven's name the maddening image of Elizabeth Fairchild kept popping into his mind. Auburn hair flying, brown eyes blazing, she galloped one moment on a mare and spun around the next moment in another man's arms on the dance floor.

At thirty-two, he was more than ready to settle down. In fact, town life held little appeal for the marquis. He would most likely have chosen not to come to London at all this year were it not for the fact that he still lacked that necessary annoyance, a wife.

Much as it might aggravate him, a wife was necessary, particularly if one preferred to live in the country, which he did. For one thing, he most certainly wanted children, and for another, he did sometimes tire of exclusively masculine company.

Now Lord Meridan was toying with the notion of marrying Ariadne Singleton. He was well aware that hers was not a spotless reputation. She had warmed his bed, and who knew how many other gentlemen might have claimed the same honour?

Yet one could not easily disregard her tall, well-formed figure, her rich chestnut hair, and those amazing aquamarine eyes. Furthermore, she had inherited a respectable fortune from her late husband. The marquis did not need her money, but it was always desirable to merge two fortunes when one could.

What was it about Ariadne that nevertheless gave him pause? Not her rather free dispersal of her favours, for she had never gone so far as to be the subject for gossip. And after all, a widow was allowed certain leeway.

Nor was it the fact that her social status was not quite as high as it might be .She was acceptable to the ton, if marginally, and as his wife there would be no question but that she would be received in the best homes.

No, it was something else, he reflected, watching idly as a group of club members strolled by on their way to the green baize tables in the spacious gaming-room.

Loyalty. He did not trust the woman. She had never led him astray, that he knew of, but then she had no reason to. Yet one married for a lifetime, and he had the uneasy feeling his charms might wear thin for her, immured in the countryside.

Tired of his own thoughts, which were leading him nowhere, his lordship roused himself enough to speak to his companion.

"You are certainly in a brown study, Percy," he said. "Come, have you gambled too deep? You know I may be counted on to help a fellow out."

Percy smiled wanly, his hazel eyes troubled. "Ah, if only lack of money were the problem."

"Now, there is a statement one is not likely to hear twice in one's lifetime," Brett observed.

Apparently his friend had lost his usually unfailing sense of humour, for he did not even smile. "You did not hear my news, then," he said.

"No, indeed. What news?"

"Good!" Percy perked up a bit. "If you have not heard it, then most likely no one else has either."

"I'm not sure I follow you, but pray tell me what this is about."

The marquis watched his comrade with concern. He had lost one dear friend with Louis Chumley's death, and Sir Percy was the only remaining gentleman of his acquaintance for whom he cared two shakes of a rat's tail.

"My inheritance," sighed Percy gloomily. "My Uncle Freddie died, and I have come into twenty thousand pounds a year."

Brett straightened in his chair, certain that his ears had deceived him. "I do not believe I understand, good fellow," he said. "Let us run through this again."

"By all means." Percy heaved yet another sigh, this one quaking his slender frame.

"Your uncle has died."

"Yes."

The marquis nodded. "I see. And you were very fond of your uncle."

"Freddie? Couldn't stand the man. Drank five bottles of port a night and had a nose as red as a furnace."

Brett searched his mind for some other explanation for his friend's gloom. "His death has perhaps left a grieving aunt, or some impoverished cousins?"

"What?" Percy stared at him as if he had taken leave of his senses. "Nonsense. Freddie was a bachelor."

"Then why the blazes are you acting so blue-deviled?" Brett burst out. "Confound it, man, explain yourself!"

They were interrupted by a cheer from the window, and could determine from the general remarks that one of the Cyprians, perhaps even Harriette Wilson herself, had passed by the club and blown a kiss at the occupants.

"Why couldn't I be like you?" Percy mused. "A happy bachelor, passing without a care from one woman's arms to another."

"There is some condition in the will, then?" Brett guessed. "You must get yourself leg-shackled within the year, perhaps?" He had heard of such bizarre demands in wills, although generally from a father rather than an uncle, particularly a drunken bachelor.

"No, no." Percy shook his head. "It is this romantic nature of mine, Brett. I cannot love a woman who will only have me for my money."

"Ah." The marquis began to understand, at least a little. "But that is the way of the world, Percy. A woman must marry as best she can, and if she has some money of her own, naturally she will not squander it on some ramshackle fellow.''

"I disagree," said Percy heatedly. "I do not think it is natural at all. A woman's inclinations should follow her heart, and her head should trail some distance behind."

"A disturbing portrait." His lordship indulged in a smile, but his friend failed to return it. "And who might be the lady in question, may I ask?"

"Why, Lady Hester, of course!" returned Percy as if there were no other woman in London worthy of consideration.

"She has heard of your inheritance, then and begun to fawn on you?" the marquis asked. "But it is only two weeks since we are arrived in town. Surely she has not even had her come-out yet."

"No." Percy draped one fawn-trousered leg over the arm of his chair. "But soon she shall hear of it, no doubt. And then I shall never have an opportunity to win her for myself. She will perhaps marry me, but it will all be for money, and so I shall never be able to feel secure in her regard."

"Now, there is a problem I know well," said Lord Meridan, and related his doubts about Ariadne.

"Yes, well, there's no doubt that she's mercenary, dear fellow," Percy agreed. "Although if that were her only motive, she might cast herself in the way of young Winston. He lies in wait for a dukedom."

"But he has already lost his heart to Lady Elizabeth, I believe." The marquis felt an odd twinge at mentioning her name. It would be awkward indeed if anyone, even Percy, ever guessed that he harboured a lingering partiality toward the woman whom he knew to be the most heartless in London.

His companion shook his head. "Not so much since she has recovered from her illness, although I have heard he still calls on her, and on Ariadne as well. He is quite taken with Mrs. Singleton, I believe."

"Indeed?" An idea was bestirring itself in the back of the marquis's mind. "One wonders how Ariadne would behave were I to lose most of my money."

"Ah, well, I am an expert on how the impecunious are treated by the ton," Percy advised him. "As a man, of course, I am welcome where a woman would not be, for we are always needed to make up a set in the quadrille or a hand at cards. And of course I may earn a fortune in some way, perhaps by exiling myself to India long enough to become a nabob trading in tea and spices. But let me assure you that the mamas do not smile when I ask their daughters to dance, and the daughters do not regard me when a man of wealth is nearby."

"Mmmm." Even as another cheer went up from the increasingly merry crowd in the bow window, the marquis found his mind humming a new tune. "I have heard of a gentleman who pretended to be dead, to learn what his family and friends truly thought of him."

"And most unpleasantly surprised he was, too," added Percy.

"Since what I most want is to retire to the country, I have little to lose, have I?" observed Brett.

Percy unwrapped his leg from the arm of his chair and faced his friend, amazement written across his countenance. "Do you mean you truly contemplate telling the world that you have become impoverished?"

"Well . . ." Brett considered the idea for a moment longer, savouring its many possibilities. "Perhaps it would be too improbable that I should suddenly lose everything."

"Indeed it would!"

"But not that I should lose a great deal. I have invested considerably in shipping, for example. It could be put about that several vessels had been sunk, without revealing any names that might disturb other investors. My acquaintance might not find it difficult to credit that I should find myself in somewhat straitened circumstances."

"And how are you to convince them of this?" inquired Percy, his face lighting up with interest and his own dismals quite forgotten.

The marquis toyed with the edges of his immaculately starched cravat. "A few discreet words to a few indiscreet people. Perhaps I shall let it be known that I seek a tenant for my estate in Kent, and a buyer for the hunting lodge in Scotland, since it is not entailed."

Percy nodded slowly. "A good enough reason to inform some of your friends of your changed status," he agreed. "Shall you tell Mrs. Singleton yourself?"

Brett shook his head. "I think not. Let her learn of my misfortune in the usual way, and then we shall see what happens. The truth will get out soon enough, when my man of affairs learns of the rumours. And how about you, my friend?"

"I shall continue as I am, so far as anyone knows," Sir Percy said. "But I must find some way to discern Hester's true feelings, mustn't I? Sooner or later my truth is likely to get about as well."

The two men mulled this difficulty for some time. Meanwhile, the men in the window appeared to have tired of their pastime, for they began to disperse.

"And what do you think of the new crop of beauties, Beau?" one of the gentlemen asked Brummel as they walked by the two seated men.

The Beau shrugged delicately. "More or less the same as last year's, I suppose. With one exception. I had not made the acquaintance of Lady Elizabeth Fairchild last season, although she was out, and I find myself most impressed with her."

"Indeed?" His companion looked at her in surprise. "She is reputed to be something of a hoyden."

"Merely an honest woman, something one rarely finds these days," said the Beau. "And a beautiful one, although not in the usual way. She is the only one worthy of notice."

They passed out of earshot. The marquis glared after them. How dare Beau Brummel praise the woman who had lured Louis Chumley to his death? He had expected the Beau, at least, to see through her pretense of sincerity.

And he did not like the notion that young bucks would be hanging out after Beth, admiring her beauty because it was the fashion to do so.

But the conversation had given Percy another idea. "Capital!" he said. "Beth will have dozens of admirers, the way the Beau is carrying on about her. And I shall become one of them." He looked to the marquis in clear expectation of approval.

"Have you taken leave of your senses?" his friend demanded. "The chit is the worst sort of opportunist. She . . ."

"That has not been my observation, but I won't disagree, since you told me about her role in the fate of poor Chumley," Percy said. "The point is, Brett, I shall be merely another face in the crowd to her, and not a desirable one because of my poverty."

"Then what is the point?" asked the marquis with a touch of peevishness.

"Ah." Percy raised a finger admonishingly. "Jealousy. I shall see then what Hester truly thinks of me. If she cares at all, she will be furious."

Brett settled back in his chair. "I salute you, Percy." He poured himself a glass of sherry from a decanter and lifted it admiringly. "You have hit on a splendid scheme."

Oddly enough, however, the marquis realised as he left the club that evening and headed for his townhouse in Cavendish Square, he was not entirely pleased to think that Percy would be sniffing around Beth Fairchild.

But why not? he scolded himself, just as another thought hit him.

His newly reduced status would reach the ears of Lady Elizabeth as well as Mrs. Singleton. And then she would show him her true colours indeed.

Lady Eleanor Fairchild had been delighted to see the pile of invitations on the sideboard in the front hall within days after her daughters' arrival in London. Routs and balls, breakfasts and card parties—what a whirl of activity lay ahead!

She had lost no time in planning Hester's come-out, so that she might profit from this popularity, but to Lady Fairchild's frustration, no suitable orchestra could be engaged for several weeks. The modistes, the flower shops, and the haberdashers as well were all too busy to serve her until almost the middle of April.

Curiously enough, the invitations did not trickle away. Indeed, they increased. And Beth was included in all of them, she saw to her astonishment.

It was Lady Frankstone who gave the game away at last. "Why, Eleanor, didn't you *know*?" she cried. "The Beau has given his stamp of approval to Elizabeth. Apparently he was most taken with her at Lady Smythe's supper party. She has become quite the thing."

"I fear I don't understand," ventured the perplexed mother. "What is there about Elizabeth that should attract anyone's notice? Beyond her occasional bad manners, of course."

Her visitor, who sat in the yellow saloon sipping tea, chuckled and rapped her lightly with a gloved hand. "Bad manners, indeed!" snorted Lady Frankstone. "The Beau calls it honesty, and it has become all the rage. Ladies are becoming downright insulting these days, telling everyone what they truly think. But it will not last, my dear, because you know, they do not truly think at all."

Lady Fairchild was inclined to discount the matter, since Lady Frankstone was well known to be something of a hoyden herself and had never disapproved of Beth as she ought. But others of her acquaintance soon confirmed the astonishing fact that Beth had somehow managed to become the latest sensation.

Her mother took to her bed for two full days, alternating between resentment that her least favourite child should be so fortunate, and pride that a daughter of hers should be the darling of society.

At the end of the time she arose, announced that her megrim was gone, and concentrated on outfitting both her daughters in the finest silks and satins, with French laces—a rarity since the war with France—and cunning Italian half-boots, and every manner of bonnet and glove, pelisse, and reticule.

As for Beth herself, she was quite stunned and not at all pleased at the number of gentlemen who came to call on her. For one thing, their manner was not sincere. They would tire of her as soon as fashion did, and so were not worth her notice.

Moreover, when she spoke to them directly, questioning their interest in her and challenging them to deny that it was solely the desire to appear a la mode, they responded by applauding her forthrightness rather than answering her.

It was frustrating indeed to be made much of, and know the admiration to be mere flattery; to speak difficult truths, and to be patted on the head like a child and told how clever one was; to welcome half the males in London to one's drawing room, and not the one man whose presence would have been welcome.

Even the Viscount Winston, who had seemed at least a sincere person, came rarely, and when he called he was as ill at ease in

Beth's company as he ever had been in Alicia's. Her memory restored, she offered little allure; and besides, tattle had it that he was smitten with the flashy Mrs. Singleton.

"What a piece of luck you have had!" Hester muttered ungraciously one afternoon when the last of the false suitors had gone. "How I would like to be in your shoes!"

"But they cannot call on you until you have come out," Beth reminded her as Hester consumed a cream cake, having been obliged to remain upstairs until the gentlemen departed.

"Still, I shall never be this sought after," Hester said. "You have had two baronets here this afternoon, and the eldest son of an earl, and one of the richest men in the city, even if he is in trade."

"But I do not care for their titles or their money," Beth told her.

"Liar!" challenged her sister, ignoring the startled look of a parlourmaid who was clearing away the teacups. "What else is there?"

"Why, the man himself," said Beth.

"Oh, I suppose." Hester squirmed down in her chair, for in her sister's presence she did not bother to maintain her ladylike facade. "But one can have both."

"Some can, perhaps." To her dismay, Beth found herself near tears, staring down into her cold tea. She remembered how it had felt to dance in the marquis's arms, to see his glowing eyes so close to her face, but now that was all gone forever.

She had disgraced herself and, worse, her misconduct had cost an innocent man his life. Yet still she remembered little of Louis Chumley, save a few superficial conversations at the opera and once when he had tried to steal a kiss at Vauxhall Gardens. There must be entire scenes blotted from her memory. How could she ever trust herself again?

"There you are." Lady Fairchild entered the room carrying several sheets of paper. "I am just reviewing the guest list for Hester's come-out. Tell me, Beth, what do you think of inviting the Arundels?"

"Why do you not ask me?" pouted Hester. "It is my debut, after all."

"But you know nothing of society," her mother dismissed her airily.

"That is not the problem at all!" Hester fumed. "It is all because of Beau Brummel, isn't it? You did not care two hoots for Beth's opinion before she had everyone at her feet!"

Lady Fairchild stared at her youngest daughter as if seeing her for the first time. "This is not the sort of behaviour I have come to expect from you, Hester."

The girl refused to take the hint, despite Beth's warning shake of the head. "You are as fickle as any male, Mother! I have always been your favourite, and look what I have sacrificed to win your esteem! Did I gallop about the countryside whenever I willed? Did I rescue dirty kittens and soil my skirts, or miss a dinner party because I had caught cold from a labourer's child, taking soup to their hovel? No! I was always the best of daughters, and now for no good reason at all I am pushed aside!"

Lady Fairchild quelled her younger daughter with a cold glare. "I do not condone Elizabeth's former misdeeds, but the fact is that she has made a place for herself in society. A fluke it may be, but she is entitled to be consulted on matters of a social nature. Whereas you, missy, from what accounts I have heard, were only a moderate success at Lady Smythe's, and that does not bode well for you at all."

From Hester's stricken look, Beth realized that her sister had been deeply hurt by their mother's rejection. Indeed, she herself was shocked that Lady Fairchild could turn so readily against her favourite.

"This is most unjust, Mother," she began, the butler knocked at the drawing room door and entered.

"There is a gentleman here, my lady, if you please," he informed them. "Sir Percy Stem."

"Aha!" Hester recovered at once, giving Beth a triumphant look. "You see, I have one admirer already, and I am not even out yet."

"Beg pardon, miss," said the butler, "but he did request to see Miss Elizabeth."

"You must go upstairs, Hester," reproved her mother, adding with a sigh, "I had hoped to have an hour or so before dinner to look over our plans. It is tiring, you know, Beth, having to chaperone you all day."

"I'm sorry, Mother." But Beth's attention was on her sister's white face. "Please let Hester stay. She and Sir Percy are already acquainted, and that way you at least may be free to carry on."

"Very well." Their mother departed through the side door as the butler was dispatched to fetch Beth's newest and very unexpected admirer.

=8=

IF SIR PERCY Stem was taken aback when he entered the room and saw Hester sitting with Beth, he revealed it only in a moment's hesitation. Then he bowed politely and presented Beth with a box of sweets, after which he positioned himself on the settee.

Hester realized that she was staring rudely, but she couldn't seem to control herself today. First she had railed at her mother, and now she sat with her mouth half open, watching Sir Percy make polite conversation with her sister.

If there was one person of whom Hester had felt secure, whom she had even taken for granted, it was Sir Percy. What a knave he was! Here he had given her to believe that his affections were engaged, and now he blew with the winds of society and came to worship at Beth's feet.

"I have been so pleased to see your success in society," he was saying just then. "I thought last year that you were unfairly overlooked, Lady Elizabeth, and I am glad to see your true worth has been discovered."

"Oh, hardly my true worth," Beth replied. "People come because I am fashionable, and if it becomes fashionable to cut me in the street, they will do that too."

"Beth is famous for her honesty, you know," Hester couldn't resist interjecting.

Percy nodded politely but kept his eyes on Beth. "I can only hope the fashion will be of long duration."

As her sister murmured an answer and the talk turned to other topics, Hester studied her two fellow players in the scene. What was

Beth thinking? How did she really feel about Percy? She gave no sign of partiality; indeed, she treated him rather as a brother or old friend than as a suitor.

Hester had to admit that Beth had changed in the last few weeks. Even her rebellious red-brown hair had been tamed by the ministrations of a new abigail, and now curled delicately about her face. Moreover, her sister's new and more modest wardrobe became her, for Beth's slender build and soft curves needed no daring necklines and damped petticoats to make them appealing.

Still, the one person Beth surely longed for had not come—the Marquis of Meridan. He had not come to see Hester either, of course, but then she was not out yet.

That must be it! she thought suddenly. Of course, Sir Percy could not come to see her openly. Perhaps his visit to Beth was merely a pretext to see Hester. Yes, that must be the explanation!

Hester brightened immediately and began to listen to the conversation. They were discussing the poem *Childe Harold*, published only that month, a topic of little interest to her since she had not read it.

"I have always been of the opinion that it does not suit a woman to be overeducated or to read overmuch, for the result is dissatisfaction with her primary duties to her husband and children," Hester commented.

The other two turned to look at her. "Why may a woman not be learned as well as accomplished in the home?" inquired Sir Percy. "It seems to me people are too quick to assume that it must be one way or the other."

This thought had never occurred to Hester, who had been merely parroting something she had once heard her mother say. "Why . . . there is not time, I suppose," she said weakly. "If a woman reads too much, she must neglect either her home or her cultivation of the womanly arts of piano playing and needlework."

"You must not speak without thinking, Hester," Beth reproved mildly. "For I think that is what you are doing. Why voice an opinion that is not your own?"

"How do you know what I'm thinking?" Hester flared. "If I don't know my own mind, nobody does!"

"You are still very young," said Sir Percy patronisingly. "When you become a bit older, get more town bronze, then I think you will cease to see the world so much in blacks and whites."

"You needn't treat me like a child!" Hester snapped.

"In point of fact, you are merely the chaperone and should not speak at all," he teased. "It is not the thing for me to converse with a young lady before her come-out."

"Oh, it's quite all right," Beth put in hastily. "You may speak with Hester all you wish, Sir Percy."

Ah, thought her sister, Beth had come to the same conclusion as to the purpose of his visit.

"But while your sister is quite charming, she is not the reason I am here," Sir Percy said, dashing Hester's hopes almost as soon as they had risen. "I thought perhaps you might agree to ride with me in Hyde Park."

"Indeed." Beth looked thoughtful. "I have not been out in the park since we arrived in London. I should like that very much, Sir Percy." Then she added quickly, "Perhaps Hester could come as well."

"I'm afraid my phaeton only seats two," he said with, in Hester's opinion, unsuitable good cheer.

"I'll just fetch my pelisse and bonnet," said Beth, rising and vanishing into the hallway, leaving the door discreetly ajar.

"What game is this?" demanded Hester as soon as she had gone. "You came to see me, in truth, did you not? Then why should you go riding with my sister?"

Percy eyed her with considerable interest. "You seem very sure that it was you I wished to see."

"But of course it is!" Hester glared at him. "It is always me you wish to see. Certainly you cannot think you have a chance with Beth? She has half of London pursuing her, and you haven't even a fortune to tempt her."

The visitor only nodded wisely, his eyes trailing along the delicate grey muslin sleeves of Hester's gown. The dress, with its high neck and gleaming pearl buttons, emphasised the vividness of Hester's blue eyes and slenderness of her arms, as she well knew, and she felt reassured.

"Furthermore, she has her cap set for someone else, I am certain," Hester went on.

"Oh?" He did look interested now. "And who might that be?"

"Why, the Marquis of Meridan, of course." Hester smiled happily. Now she had cooked Beth's goose for sure.

Sir Percy shook his head glumly. "Such a shame about Brett. One would never have thought it would happen to him, of all men."

"What would happen?" Hester leaned forward eagerly. "Oh, do tell me. I'm always the last to know everything."

"You mean you haven't heard about his run of ill luck?" Sir Percy gazed at her in astonishment. "Good Lord, I thought . . . well, no matter, you'd hear it soon enough anyway. A number of his investments have come a cropper these past few months, and he finds himself in considerably straitened circumstances."

"How straitened?" Hester demanded.

Sir Percy shrugged. "I'm afraid I don't know the whole of it, but it appears he's seeking a tenant for his estate. I believe his family has a small establishment in Cornwall, and perhaps he will retire there."

"Cornwall!" Hester gasped. "Oh, Sir Percy, I'm so glad you told me. I might have made the most grievous error . . . but never mind, I'm safe now."

"Grievous error?" he inquired with some spirit. "I was not aware you and the marquis were that well acquainted."

"Indeed, our families are neighbours," she sniffed. "And I had always thought . . . but of course this changes everything."

"I thought it might," Sir Percy said ambiguously.

"Beg pardon?"

Beth returned then, and Hester felt a rush of sympathy for her. As for herself, her interest in the marquis had been purely a rational reaction to his title and his wealth, but she suspected that her sister had lost her heart some time ago. And now he would be beyond consideration. She considered blurting the news, but Sir Percy had already risen, given a cursory bow, and begun leading his companion out the door.

From the window, Hester watched them emerge into the late afternoon sunshine of Berkeley Square. In spite of herself, she yearned to yank the windowpanes open and throw something heavy at them.

Sir Percy might not be a suitable husband, but by rights he belonged to Hester!

The memory of their dance together at Lady Smythe's swept over her with a wave of pain. He had looked at her so meltingly, touched her so tenderly, that she had dreamed about him for nights afterward. And now she was ignored and cast aside.

Well, he would see. Once Hester came out, she would be the rage of London, too. And she would have nothing to do with the smug and arrogant Sir Percy Stem.

The weather was delightful for late March, and Beth found herself enjoying the ride much more than she had anticipated as the handsome pair of matched bays turned into Hyde Park.

It was just going five, the fashionable hour, and the park was full of carriages—calashes and chaises, phaetons and landaus. And each carriage was full of finely dressed ladies and gentlemen, while still others rode about on horses.

"What a parade it is," said Sir Percy. "All decked out in their finery, putting on a show for one another."

Beth smiled. "It is a lovely spectacle if one can appreciate it for what it is. Last year, I was too wrapped up in my own worries."

"And what were they, may I ask?" He guided the horses around a carriage that had stopped to take up an acquaintance.

"Oh, strange as it seems to me now, I was all in a muddle about not being a la mode," she admitted. "Partly I wanted so badly to please my mother, but I think I've accepted now that that isn't possible."

"What a sad commentary." Percy regarded her gravely. "My family was always a bit down on its luck, but we were happy."

Beth leaned back in her seat in the high-perch vehicle, enjoying the view and the easy companionship of Sir Percy. His lack of fortune might trouble Hester, but given that each girl had a competence of her own, it would not have worried Beth. However, she knew quite well that her feelings for Sir Percy were of the platonic variety.

Soon Beth and Sir Percy were spotted by the others, and their phaeton was surrounded by carriages and horsemen. She had the distinct feeling that her embroidered gown of lilac muslin, with a discreet circlet of pearls at the throat, was being much scrutinised and would be discussed in great detail moments later.

Both Beth and Sir Percy made an effort to join in the general chitchat, but it was difficult to communicate from a distance and frankly she found the ton rather wearying these days.

As soon as he could, Sir Percy disentangled them and headed into the Serpentine, where they might continue with a little more peace.

"I find it sad that now when I have what I so longed for last year, it no longer matters," Beth sighed.

Again, Sir Percy studied her earnestly. "And what does matter?"

As if in answer to the question, she glanced up to see another stylish phaeton, this one pulled by a handsome team of ebony horses and lacquered in black and ivory. Riding high on its seats were Lord Meridan and Mrs. Singleton.

"So they are together again," she observed, almost without realising she had spoken.

Sir Percy turned the horses so the two vehicles would intersect. In a moment, both he and the marquis had halted their teams and were greeting each other warmly. The marquis favoured Beth with only a stiff bow, and she felt her spirits sink.

"I fear you will shame us all, Lady Elizabeth," called Ariadne with feigned gaiety, her eyes quickly taking in Beth's dress. "You are setting a pattern for simplicity that few of us can wear to advantage." Her own gown was of blue velvet, too warm for the day and revealing an unusual expanse of bosom.

"You are very kind," Beth called back, for once holding her tongue.

Ariadne smiled, although there was no warmth in her eyes. "Do promise you will call upon me tomorrow in Clarence Square. I must have your opinion on some plans of mine for a masked ball, and I assure you that your participation will guarantee its success."

"I am hardly the one to advise you about a masked ball," Beth returned, uneasy at the prospect of more intimate acquaintance with this intimidating woman. "I am celebrated for my unmasking, you know."

"How clever!" Ariadne uttered a short, tinkling laugh that to Beth's ears sounded well-practised. "But you will come, won't you?"

There was no way round it without making a direct cut. "Of course," she said, wondering why Ariadne was so set on this meeting.

Throughout this exchange, Lord Meridan had watched the two ladies wordlessly. Beth noticed that he gave Sir Percy one quizzical look, and she sensed a faint shaking of her companion's head in response. Now whatever could that mean?

The two parties separated, much to Beth's relief. "I wish she had not asked me," she confessed as soon as they were out of hearing. "I do not feel comfortable with the woman."

"She is not among my favourites, either," said Sir Percy. "But Brett appears quite taken with her, wouldn't you say?"

"I hadn't noticed." And she hadn't, Beth thought, because she hadn't dared look at him, although the mere fact of his taking the woman driving surely indicated far more commitment than she would wish.

"Well, it is too bad about him," said Sir Percy.

"Oh, surely she cannot be such a poor bargain as all that," Beth returned.

Her friend chuckled. "I did not mean because of Ariadne Singleton. No, no, I was speaking of his ill luck with his investments."

Beth frowned. "I had heard nothing of this," she said. "He is not despondent, surely?" It had been difficult to tell anything of the marquis's mood, she realised now.

"Oh, Brett never displays his emotions," Sir Percy commented. "But I fear he has lost the better part of his fortune."

"Then surely as his friend you should not be so eager to spread the word," Beth chastised.

He looked startled for a moment, and then nodded in agreement. "I had thought it was general knowledge already."

"Not to me," said Beth, and wondered if Ariadne knew of this turn of affairs.

"Well, now that I am begun, I had well as not finish, hadn't I?" Sir Percy clucked to the horses, which were showing signs of taking an interest in the thick leaves of the shrubbery.

"It is my impression that there will be no stopping you," said Beth. "Very well. Go on."

"He has had a good many set-backs," said Sir Percy. "Ships sunk and all that. Severely straitened circumstances as a result.

Plans to let his estate in Kent, I believe, and retire to Cornwall."

"But he has a home in London as well," Beth pointed out. "There is no disgrace in having one's investments turn out ill, so surely he need not flee to the countryside. It is not as if he had wasted his inheritance on gambling."

Sir Percy sighed, and she wondered if somehow she had missed the point. "Yes, but don't you see, a man like Brett, he could not bear to remain in London and see doors closed to him and friends turn away."

"Friends would not turn away," said Beth. "You did not, just now, did you?"

"Not me, of course." Her companion pursed his lips reflectively.

"And surely not so many doors would be closed to him," Beth continued. "Begging your pardon, Sir Percy, but your pockets have always been more or less to let, and no one has snubbed you." Oh, dear, she thought, that was rather bold of me, and perhaps rather rude as well.

However, Sir Percy did not appear to take offense. "That is a different matter altogether," he said heavily, as though plowing through unturned earth. "My relationships have been established on quite a different basis. Brett is used to holding a position of authority, of prestige, whereas I am satisfied to take what scraps I can."

"Well," said Beth, "I will consider the marquis a great coward if he chooses to run away. He has done nothing wrong, and at least he will know now who his true friends are." Then she added thoughtfully, "Does Mrs. Singleton know, do you think?"

Sir Percy shrugged. "Who can say? But tell me, Lady Elizabeth, how could a woman not change her opinion of a man when his circumstances are so changed? After all, her style of living must be determined by the wealth of the man she marries."

"Pray do not press me on the subject, for I will quite bore you with my answer," Beth told him as she gazed thoughtfully across the park at the clusters of carriages, the flower-bright array of gowns floating through the spring afternoon.

"Can you not give me a clew?" inquired Sir Percy. "As to the nature of your answer, that is?"

"I would prate on tediously about my sister Mary, and her happy life in the country with her husband and small ones, and how little fine clothes and townhouses signify if one cannot have the man one loves." It occurred to Beth that she had perhaps come too close to a dangerous confession. "So I would imagine that any woman who truly valued a man—such as your friend—would not be swayed by his change in fortune."

Sir Percy nodded thoughtfully and spoke hardly at all for the rest of their drive.

Beth was surprised to learn, on her return home, that her mother had already been apprised of Lord Meridan's ill fortune.

"Who would have suspected such a thing?" Lady Fairchild cried as she and Hester lounged in Beth's sitting room, watching her dress for dinner.

"Certainly he gave no sign of it to us, did he, Lizzie?" asked Hester. "I hope you are not too horribly disappointed."

"Disappointed?" Beth turned to her, rather annoying the abigail who was arranging her hair with the aid of a curling iron. "Why should I be?"

"Don't play sly with us, Lizzie," reproved their mother. "You cannot deny you had certain hopes in that direction."

There was no use pretending otherwise, and besides, Beth began to think she had forgotten how to dissemble. "I suppose I did."

"And so did I, of course," admitted Hester with uncharacteristic directness. "It is too bad for you the viscount has transferred his affections elsewhere, although they may not yet be fixed."

"The viscount is a young puppy and would not suit," Beth replied, marveling at how her unruly hair submitted meekly to the abigail's ministrations. "Besides, I do not understand your condolences, Hester. The marquis never took any interest in me."

Lady Fairchild smiled knowingly. "That is not what Hester told me. A matter of a certain ki—" She stopped midword as she remembered that abigails had ears as well as hands. "A certain friendship between the two of you, I meant to say."

"The marquis never cared two shakes for me," Beth answered with hard-won composure. "If he had, I should certainly not be swayed by his loss of fortune."

"What!" Both women gasped at once.

"Surely you would not even consider . . ." began Lady Fairchild.

"You couldn't possibly think of . . ." Hester started to say.

"I most certainly would and could," Beth said, stepping into the brown satin gown the abigail held for her. "But it is all nonsense now. In fact, I am bid to call upon my successful rival tomorrow, if you must know. Mrs. Singleton has urged me to call on her."

"That trollop!" sniffed Lady Fairchild. "You should have cut her, Beth."

"Indeed, I could not, for it would have been public, and that would have meant an open quarrel," Beth said, knowing her mother could not disagree. "Will you come with me? I do not relish the task."

"I fear I cannot," said her mother. "Hester and I must search out the material for her ball. And you must have a new gown, too."

"The modiste has my measure." Beth waved her hand airily. "Choose something simple, will you, Mother? I am so weary of those endless fittings."

Hester gaped open-mouthed. "I do not understand this change in you at all."

Lady Fairchild's face settled into a frown. "Your sister cannot bear to be approved of," she said. "She must always be contrary. You would think the envy of others were a thing to be despised. She takes pleasure from thinking that half London will admire her taste for a gown she did not even care to choose herself."

Beth turned to stare at them both. "I am not being contrary on purpose, Mother. But . . . oh, how can I explain it? Never mind. Let us go down to dinner, shall we?"

Before either could protest, she pulled her mother and sister to their feet and spirited them out the door ahead of her.

Perhaps, Beth reflected sadly, she should ask to be sent to Mary's for the rest of the season. She simply could not face watching the marquis and knowing he would never be hers, nor could she take pleasure in her own success, knowing that her excesses of the previous year had cost a young man's life.

Or had they? This one remaining gap in her memory puzzled her immensely. Perhaps, before she gave up on London entirely, she should make an attempt to find out what had really happened with Louis Chumley.

Mrs. Singleton had been a close friend of Lord Meridan's the previous year, when he had been well acquainted with Mr. Chumley. Perhaps she had observed some details that might aid in spurring Beth's recall.

She nodded to herself as they joined her father in the dining room. The next day's visit might not be entirely wasted, after all.

=== 9 ===

MRS. ARIADNE SINGLETON'S house was at a fashionable address, presenting a tidy brick facade that looked upon the rose garden in Clarence Square.

The very normality of the house reassured Beth somewhat as she descended from the family carriage with her maid, who would remain in the background throughout the visit.

A stiffly proper butler answered the door, and Beth was ushered into a drawing room decorated in the airy Regency style, with soft blue hues in the cloth panels upon the wall and delicate chairs, sofas, and tables that hinted of Greek classical lines.

As she waited for her hostess, Beth studied the room. Despite the lightness of the decorations, she had the feeling of a fly trapped inside a spider's web. What nonsense that was!

Yet in this room she sensed the presence of others who had visited here. Louis Chumley, perhaps; his ghost might be watching her even now. She shivered.

And the Marquis of Meridan. The previous season, it had been rumoured—but only in discreet whispers—that he was Ariadne's lover. Had he come here then? Surely he attended her now, for the two went driving together.

What did a lover do, precisely? Beth tried to imagine the marquis holding Mrs. Singleton in his arms, but the picture was too painful to tolerate. It was with a sense of relief that she heard the drawing room door open.

"I am so glad you could come!" cried Ariadne. She moved forward with hands outstretched and Beth was obliged to accept her grip for a moment. "And I am delighted to be able to chat with you alone!"

The maid gave no sign of taking offense at being thus disregarded in her corner, and Beth accepted a seat on a small gilt chair.

"I hope the drawing room is not too formal?" said Ariadne. "We should remove to the green saloon, but the light in here is so delightful in the mornings."

"Yes, it is," Beth agreed, trying not to focus on her hostess' skin, whose roughness showed clearly beneath her paint in the drapery-filtered sunshine. She was pleased to see at least that Mrs. Singleton had worn a simple cherry muslin dress with an almost modest scooped neckline.

Ariadne had apparently followed her gaze, for she said in confiding tones, "You see how your style has influenced us all, dear Elizabeth? Simplicity and youthfulness, those are the watchwords!"

Beth shook her head, folding her hands in the rose-sprigged muslin of her skirt. "It was not my aim to set any modes, I assure you, madam."

"Ariadne." Again the warm smile. "I simply insist that you call me by my given name."

"Of course." The conversation broke off as two maids brought in a silver tea service and a plate of cakes.

Ariadne looked thoughtful after their departure. "Do you suppose your maid would prefer to join them in the kitchen? Of course she is welcome to stay here, but we might speak more freely."

Beth remembered her own questions about Mr. Chumley and nodded. The maid was only too pleased to remove to the relative informality of the kitchen, and soon they were alone.

"It has struck me that perhaps you had some matters to discuss with me, other than the masked ball," Beth said as Ariadne poured tea. "Pray speak your mind."

Her hostess bided her time as she served Beth a steaming cup of the fragrant liquid. It struck Beth that Ariadne was more likely choosing what facade to present than which words to use.

"It is only that I wish to be friends," Ariadne answered at last.

Beth could not help reflecting that she would as soon be friends with a hungry lioness. But she kept silent.

"As you know, your name is on everyone's tongue these days," Mrs. Singleton continued. "A widow like me, so many years out of style, can only hope to bask a little in your reflected glory."

"Oh, do let us be frank." Beth set her teacup and saucer upon the side table, afraid she might gag. "You need no one's reflected glory, Mrs. Singleton. You are escorted by one of the most eligible man in London, and you are still very beautiful." The last was not perhaps entirely true, in Beth's eyes, but she was well aware that the other woman's sophistication and blatant sensuality more than compensated in most men's eyes for her lack of freshness.

"Nevertheless, it would benefit us both to be friends," Ariadne pressed. "There is much of the ways of society that you do not know, and that may yet trip you up. And as I say, I am rather old news to the ton."

She wants to keep an eye on me, Beth thought, and could not help smiling.

"Do I amuse you?" Mrs. Singleton watched her carefully.

She shook her head. "No, it is only . . . I laugh at society, that it makes much of me. You see, Mrs. Singleton, last year when I wanted acclaim, I could not have it. This year, I am changed, and want only a simple life, and what do I find? Dandies at my doorstep!"

The wariness had not left Ariadne's face. "No one despises society's admiration, Lady Elizabeth."

Clearly her hostess would never understand how Beth felt, but this seemed a good opportunity to bring up her own questions. "The fact is that I am rather dismayed by my own behaviour of last year," she said.

"Why?" Mrs. Singleton gazed at her wide-eyed over the rim of her teacup. "You were quite merry and lively. I'm sure everyone thought you enchanting."

Beth shrugged. "Not everyone. Particularly not my mother, but that is neither here nor there. Ariadne, did you know Louis Chumley?"

The other woman's jaw tightened. "Slightly."

"I remember him scarcely at all," Beth said, fingering one of the cakes and nibbling at it absentmindedly before continuing. "The trouble is, I lost my memory after my fall, and parts of it have still not come back to me."

"How very interesting." Ariadne relaxed. "That must be awkward for you."

Beth nodded. "But the worst of it is, I have been told that I toyed with Mr. Chumley's affections and broke his heart, and drove him to depart on a ship that sank. So it seems I must be responsible for his death, yet I remember knowing him only slightly. It was my impression it was my inheritance that drew him, not my person."

Her hostess sat back on the sofa, apparently in deep contemplation. "I have heard something of this," she admitted. "It was what Louis himself told several of his friends, that you had broken his heart, and I cannot imagine why he would manufacture such a story. Yet in truth I never saw the two of you together, so I cannot enlighten you as to your conduct."

Beth's face must have reflected her disappointment, for Ariadne added quickly, "But young men's hearts are broken all the time. It is surely not your fault that he chose so drastic a measure as fleeing to America, and no one can say you had anything to do with sinking the ship."

Beth smiled reluctantly. "That may be. But I cannot excuse myself."

"Do not refine upon it too much." Ariadne leaned forward confidingly. "We women are always much too hard upon ourselves. Let us make plans for this costume ball of mine, and soon you will forget your troubles."

For the next half-hour, they chatted amiably, the older woman high-spirited and gay; however, Beth could not help but be on her guard. The ball was to be held at the beginning of May, they decided, and the theme was to be figures from history.

"I shall ask the Marquis of Meridan to be my host. Do you not think that a good idea?" Despite the casual tone, Beth could tell her hostess was scrutinising her for her reaction.

"He should be delighted," she replied evenly. "It is clear that he favours you, Ariadne."

"Oh, do you think so?" The woman's smile bordered on pure

gloating. "Or perhaps it would be even better if we held the ball at his house. It is much larger than mine, and as a single man he should be glad of the chance to entertain without having to plan it himself."

His house. Yes, Ariadne would like that. To be the marquis's hostess in his home was to all but announce that they were betrothed.

"Yet, perhaps the expense at this time . . ." Beth hesitated, wondering how much Ariadne knew.

"Expense?" the woman regarded her curiously. "How do you mean? Brett is immensely wealthy."

"Indeed," Beth murmured. "I—I am sure I spoke out of turn. It is not my custom to spread gossip."

Ariadne's tone sharpened. "If there is any gossip that concerns Brett, I have a right to know of it. Who told you this news?"

"Sir Percy Stem," Beth admitted, and heard a quick intake of breath.

"Then it must be true." A harshness transformed Ariadne's face as she urged, "Tell me at once, Elizabeth. What about the expense?"

"Sir Percy said that Lord Meridan has had some severe financial reverses," Beth said, realising that much as she despised spreading rumours, she was already in too thick to pull back now. "Several ships have sunk, I believe, in which he had invested heavily. So he finds himself in somewhat straitened circumstances."

"How straitened?" Ariadne demanded.

Beth picked up her cup and stared miserably into the cold dregs. "He is seeking a tenant for his estate in Kent and thinks of retiring to his property in Cornwall."

Ariadne stood up and paced the length of the room. As she turned and the morning light fell across her face, Beth had the impression of an angry vulture.

"He told me not a word!" Ariadne fumed. "No doubt he thought to marry me and make up his losses with my fortune!"

It was Beth's impulse to defend his lordship, for she could not imagine him stooping to such a tactic, but she saw at once that she had better hold herself out of this matter.

Ariadne continued pacing, pausing only when the butler came in to announce a visitor. Fearing that it might be the marquis himself, Beth rose and began to excuse herself.

"No, wait." Ariadne turned to the butler. "Do not stand about gawking like a schoolboy. Who is it?"

"The Viscount Winston," he said impassively.

Instantly, Ariadne's face cleared. "Show him in at once," she said.

Beth wished herself well away, but she did not want to make a scene. She nodded politely to the young man as he entered timidly, and noted his astonishment at seeing her there.

"You two are acquainted, are you not?" said Ariadne blithely. "Do come in, John. I am so glad to see you."

"Thank you, madam." He perched uneasily on a sofa and kept silent until a maid had been summoned and replaced the cold tea with hot.

"Had I realised you were entertaining . . ." the young man began.

"You mean Beth?" cried Ariadne, a bit too shrilly. "Oh, we are old friends. You are not disturbing us."

Once again, Beth had the feeling her hostess was studying her closely. She wants to see if I have any hold over him, she thought.

The viscount seemed on the point of suffocating from his own embarrassment, so Beth spoke at last. "I hope that you and I may be considered old friends as well, my lord. You were most considerate after my injury, but now of course I am almost completely recovered."

"Glad to hear it," he said, and cleared his throat nervously.

"Oh, I thought you had seen each other recently," Ariadne crowed, trying without success to mask her delight.

"Only a few times since my family has arrived in London," Beth informed her. "Naturally, the viscount has been occupied here in town, and I am no longer such a fascinating invalid." She gave the viscount a reassuring smile, and was pleased to see him settle back and begin to enjoy his tea.

Her way smoothed, Ariadne launched into a stream of gay tittle-tattle, keeping the viscount amused with her account of a trip to the opera and the foibles of the many peculiar people one saw there. "And of course you will come to my ball!" she exclaimed, although Beth noticed she did not go so far as to invite him to be host. "Lady Elizabeth and I have planned the most exquisite affair! But it will simply not be complete if you are not there. Oh, do say you'll come! You shall be the handsomest man in the room, I am certain of it."

John Winston, overcome by her flattery, stammered that of course he would attend.

It was becoming increasingly evident to Beth that the gangly young viscount had gained immensely in desirability to Ariadne since the news of the marquis's downfall. A dukedom at stake, she thought, shuddering inside at the thought of Ariadne as a duchess.

She finally managed to excuse herself, retrieve her maid, and depart, but her thoughts remained in a tangle and she ordered the carriage to drive round a bit so she could think matters out before returning home.

Ariadne had turned against the marquis with surprising speed when she learned of his reversals, yet Beth could not help thinking that the woman might change her mind after further thought. He remained a tremendously attractive man—she had to force her own thoughts away from the longing that spread through her at the memory of him bending over her sickbed, tenderness glowing on his face.

Still, a duke was better than a marquis if one were hanging out for a title, and John Winston was easy prey for a woman of Ariadne's skills. Moreover, Ariadne would certainly not relent if she were truly convinced the marquis had meant to use her for her money.

Then there was the matter of Ariadne's attitude toward Beth. Her concern indicated she considered the younger girl a rival, but Beth could not imagine why. True, she was much sought after just now, but she doubted it would last long. Clearly the marquis had no interest in her, nor did the young viscount.

Review the morning's conversation as she might, Beth could see no way that Ariadne could harm her. There was no man who might be taken away, and Beth's misconduct toward Louis Chumley was already well established, since he had evidently told several people of it.

Still, Beth could not put out of her mind the image of a spider-web, and a glistening spider lurking in the center of it. The difference was that now the prey was not Elizabeth Fairchild but John Winston.

Impulsively, she leaned out of the carriage window and ordered the coachman to take her to the Tonquin residence a few streets away.

She was welcomed there by two puzzled ladies. The noon hour was not a popular one for visiting, and furthermore, Beth had never before called upon Mrs. and Miss Tonquin without her own mother present.

"Perhaps I may seem a bit forward in coming here," she told them as soon as they were seated in the morning room. "However, I have some information that may be of interest to you."

"Indeed?" Alicia toyed with her needlework. "We are grateful for your condescension. One does not expect to receive in one's own house the leader of society."

"Alicia!" reproached her mother. "Envy does not become a young girl."

Beth studied Alicia for a moment, taking in her striking black hair and vivid dark eyes. What a beauty she would be, if only she didn't spoil it with her pouting and her pettiness.

"I have been to visit Mrs. Singleton this morning," Beth continued. "The Viscount Winston was a caller while I was there."

Alicia gasped. "You come here to tell me that? You can hardly expect my thanks!"

"Alicia, do hush!" snapped her exasperated mother. Beth sympathised with the poor woman, who no doubt these past few weeks had begun to see that her exquisite daughter might spoil her opportunities in society with her selfish temperament.

"It seems that Mrs. Singleton and Lord Meridan have had a falling out," Beth continued, avoiding any necessity to spread further word of the marquis's difficulties. "It was my impression that she intends to transfer her interest to Lord Winston. It is also my impression that this is not in his best interest."

Alicia had stopped playing with her yarns and was staring at her mistrustfully. "So why do you not take him away yourself, then, since he has such a fancy for you?" She ignored her mother's shocked glare.

"First of all, his fancy for me has waned considerably since I am not longer of medical concern," Beth told her quietly. "Furthermore, I have no interest beyond friendship in the viscount, and I . . . have seen enough of heartbreak to know that to win his affections under false pretenses would be no kindness."

"You are very generous to come and tell us this," Mrs. Tonquin said. "We were not aware that his courtship of Mrs. Singleton had met with any success. Naturally, it is understandable that a young man so newly come down from Oxford should wish to have his flirtations before settling down"—she glanced meaningfully at her daughter—"but I doubt that Ariadne Singleton will give him time enough to come to his senses."

"I cannot stop him from chasing after any skirt that passes by!" cried Alicia. "Do not look at me so, Mother! What does Lizzie expect me to do?"

"Tell me something," said Beth. "Do you truly care for him, or is it only his money and his title that attract you?"

"Naturally, it is his person . . ." began Mrs. Tonquin, but was waved into silence by her daughter.

"At first it was only his title that drew me," Alicia said fiercely. "I thought him an awkward young whelp, and in some ways he is. But . . ." She gnawed her lower lip for a moment before continuing. "Oh, very well, after he seemed to transfer his affections to you, Lizzie, I began to see that he is rather attractive."

"But would he continue to seem that way, if you had no rivals?"

Alicia nodded slowly. "Already he has gained a little town bronze, and I can see that he will be handsome in a few years. I do not profess to be in love with him, and I do not deny that I should adore to be a duchess and have everyone curtsey to me. But he is a steady man, and will be a good father, and he is the best man I am likely to find."

The answer satisfied Beth. True, the viscount might find some shy lady who would swoon with passion for him. But he had shown that his taste ran to more sought after women, and among them, Alicia was the most likely to make him a good wife.

"You would be well advised then to acquaint him with her reputation," Beth said. "You must open his eyes before it is too late. And now I think I had better go."

Alicia escorted her to the front door. "I apologise for my attitude when you first arrived," she said, struggling to get out the words. "I thought . . . it was all because of John I was so rude. I thought it was you he fancied."

"Rest assured, I am no threat to you," Beth answered as she departed.

She had little time to think about Ariadne Singleton or John Winston in the new few weeks, for her time was taken up with preparations for Hester's come-out.

The girl proved increasingly difficult to deal with, as Sir Percy Stem continued to call upon Beth from time to time. Yet it was not lost upon Elizabeth that his eyes sometimes strayed to her sister when Hester's attention was focussed elsewhere.

Their father, as was his custom, remained aloof, busy with his club and his newspapers. Lady Fairchild supervised the household with an iron hand, determined that all should go well for her youngest daughter's debut.

The continuing stream of visitors, cards, and flowers for Beth brought her mother's good will with them. But the recipient of all this effusive attention found herself profoundly uncomfortable. This admiration was false, and would end soon; all she could do was wait for the ax to fall.

As for Lord Meridan, she saw him only a few times, at the theatre and when she rode with one or another admirer in Hyde Park. He sometimes accompanied Ariadne, who, as Beth had suspected, had not wanted to break off all acquaintance with this devastating man.

The marquis did no more than bow stiffly to Beth yet, try as she might, she could not find another man on whom she wanted to bestow her affections.

The moment she had been dreading came the day of Hester's ball. It was Lady Frankstone who brought the news to Lady Fairchild, who in turn brought it to her daughter.

Beth was in her sitting room examining her new dress, a gossamer gown of lemon yellow overlaid with a silvery lace. Cunning little fleur-de-lis had been woven into the lace itself, and Beth fingered one of them thoughtfully, reflecting on the toil and artistry of the weaver.

She greeted her mother absentmindedly, and then noticed the frosty grimness about her mouth and eyes.

"What is it, Mother?" Beth asked.

Lady Fairchild did not even sit down. "Beau Brummel has openly insulted the Prince Regent. He is fallen entirely from favour and so, I believe, is anyone whose position rests solely on his esteem."

The delicate silver lace seemed to burn against Beth's hand. It was no use protesting that she herself had never sought the Beau's approval. Society did not regard such nice points.

"Shall I plead illness tonight?" she asked wearily. "It would be better for Hester, perhaps."

"Oh, no, you shall not," snapped her mother. "You must stand with the rest of the family to greet our guests, if there are any. This is your disgrace, Elizabeth, and you will not leave the rest of us to face it alone."

She swept out, leaving her daughter to reflect once again that no matter how she conducted herself, she had a rare talent for bringing disaster upon her own head.

Oh, well, thought Elizabeth as she laid the dress aside. At least things really cannot get much worse.

BETH TRIED NOT to think about this latest catastrophe as she checked with the cook about her daughter, a cripple for whom Beth bought paints and canvas. The girl had some artistic talent and was able to sell her small paintings for much needed income.

The girl was in high spirits, the cook told her, and even had a suitor—news that pleased and depressed Beth at the same time.

She also stopped to ask one of the parlourmaids about her ailing mother, and was reassured that the food and medicine Beth had sent earlier that week were already showing good effect.

Compared to these troubles, Beth told herself sternly, of what significance were her own woes? Yet she still quailed inwardly at the image of her family, waiting in icy formality outside the ball-room, while not a single carriage stopped in front of the house.

Her fears turned out to be singularly ill-founded. London existed largely on gossip and scandal and, as a result, a huge crush turned out for the evening's entertainment. Some of the guests, to the best of Beth's recollection, had not even been invited.

Ariadne was among the first to come, and among the most gushingly sympathetic. She lingered at the head of the stairs, where the family waited to greet the visitors.

"I was deeply distressed to hear of your ill fortune," she assured Beth.

"Very kind of you, but I do not consider it an ill fortune," Beth returned, uncomfortably aware that her guest was wearing a deep-slashed, damped gown of silver and midnight blue. It had not taken long to oust the fashion for simplicity.

"Beg pardon?" Ariadne stared as if she could not have heard correctly. "Not an ill fortune?"

"Not at all," said Beth. "This fuss over me has been artificial and therefore unwelcome. Now I shall learn who my true friends are."

"A dangerous proposition," murmured Ariadne before reluctantly giving way to another eager visitor.

Each lady seemed more anxious than the last to quiz Beth on this supposedly painful topic, to take away some word of her unhappiness with which to regale the others.

Lady Fairchild remained grimly polite, and Hester had retreated into simpers and silence. Lord Fairchild, if he were aware that disgrace of the more superficial sort had descended upon his family, appeared to regard it as yet one more annoyance to be got through.

As for Beth, she found herself feeling more and more at ease. She was discovering that she preferred to see the ton in its true colours.

"The solicitude of our many friends is most heartening," she told one lady who refused to stir until she had some words from Beth with which to amuse her friends later. "Naturally we shall be happy to have our opinions confirmed, as to who is sincere and who is false."

"And how may you determine that?" inquired the woman curiously.

"Why, by seeing who continues to call upon us and include us in their invitations," Beth said. "Perhaps it would prove amusing to create an actual list, that we and others may see how people have shown themselves."

The woman moved away uncomfortably.

"I do not see how you can be so jolly," snapped Hester under her breath as they waited for an aging dowager countess to ascend the stairs.

"Disgrace comes naturally to me," Beth replied. "I expect it was popularity I had a hard time dealing with."

Not all those in the crowd revelled in her downfall. Lady Frankstone was outspoken in her disgust for society's vagaries, and Sir

Percy gazed directly into Beth's eyes as he requested her permission to continue to call upon her, which she readily granted.

At last the painful task of providing a welcome was ended and the family was freed to join the dancing. Neither Hester nor Beth was left on the sidelines, for Sir Percy and other genuine family friends would not ignore them. In addition, attendance carried an obligation to other gentlemen to take their turn with the hostesses.

Beth tried not to refine on the fact that Lord Meridan had not come. It was unlike him to pay heed to silly scandals; most likely he had withdrawn due to his own troubles. But his apparent refusal to be a guest in their home only underscored his longstanding disdain for Beth.

As she busied herself supervising the servants and making sure the guests were plentifully supplied with refreshment, Beth watched the merrymaking with a sceptical eye.

So gay they looked, the ladies in their costly, bright gowns and the gentlemen in the well-tailored clothing that reflected Beau Brummel's influence even as his name was maligned.

Together, they formed a tapestry of gold and silver threads, woven, as most tapestries were, of the tears and toil of the less fortunate.

Last year, Beth had seen only the glitter and gaiety. True, she had always known that servants such as Sam and Mrs. Archbold laboured long hours to keep the horses fresh and the household running smoothly. And she had never been insensitive to the suffering of such unfortunates as the cook's daughter and the parlourmaid's mother.

But she had never realised so clearly the cruelty of these noble people to their own kind. The men were not so coarse as to spurn Hester at her own come-out ball, but their cold politeness as they danced with her was almost as cruel. And the ladies giggled freely together behind their fans, watching as the girl who bested most of them in looks and grace forced herself to keep her chin up.

Beth's heart went out to her sister. She had not meant to bring this unhappiness upon her. Perhaps someday it would pass. Hester was beautiful and wealthy; she would have suitors, although perhaps not as many nor as distinguished as she would have wished.

But as Beth well remembered from her own debut, the pain would take a far longer time to fade. She did not dare even look at her mother. Not only had Beth managed this time—although through no fault of her own—to land herself in a tangle, she had brought Hester down with her as well.

The gentlemen were far more attentive to Alicia Tonquin, and she knew that fact must chafe her sister even more. But Alicia clearly took no delight in her triumph. Her gaze returned again and again to the Viscount Winston who, after an obligatory turn on the dance floor with his hostesses, was hanging doggedly about Ariadne Singleton.

"Lovely ball," observed Lady Smythe from somewhere close to Beth's left ear, drawing attention to her large, lavender-clad figure and matching, bejewelled turban. "Too bad about the Beau. And to think I had him at my own house! I must have taken leave of my senses."

"You were thrilled at the time, as I recall," Beth reminded her. "It seemed then that you regarded his visit as something on the order of a favour."

Lady Smythe glared at her. "You cannot think to drag me down with you, missy! I've not been setting myself up as a leader of society."

"Well, if anyone has been setting me up, it hasn't been myself," Beth said. "It seems to me that you all enjoy positioning the pigeons of the season, purely for the joy of shooting them down. Perhaps as a sport it could replace foxhunting. At least it does not involve tearing up the farmers' fields in the course of the hunt."

"Well!" Richly offended and eager to share this latest titbit, Lady Smythe moved her portly bulk away.

To Beth's relief, her position was taken by the always reliable Lady Frankstone. "The vultures descend," she observed, watching Lady Smythe's departure. "How little they understand the laws of nature."

"Beg pardon?" asked Beth.

"The fox eats the rabbit, and the snake kills the fox," declared the older woman. "There is always a stronger predator lurking somewhere about."

Beth smiled. "All the same, I had just as soon not be the rabbit."

She stopped speaking as a tall, imposing figure paused at the far entrance to the ballroom. Lord Meridan. He had come too late to be formally received, as the family grouping had now dispersed, but the fact that he had come at all was what mattered.

"Glad to see he's put in an appearance," Lady Frankstone said stoutly. "Not the type to spurn his old friends in their time of trouble. Though from what people are saying, he's having trouble enough of his own."

Lady Fairchild had already reached the entrance and was greeting the marquis warmly. She was followed within moments by Ariadne Singleton.

That lady had been enjoying herself immensely, and now the one missing jewel had been restored to her tiara. Smiling, she accepted the marquis's request of a dance, and let herself be led out onto the floor.

"Quite a crush tonight," observed his lordship stiffly as they moved through a quadrille. "I had feared that Brummel's downfall might frighten some of them away."

"Nonsense." Ariadne pressed lightly against him, hoping the reminder of their former intimacies would fill him with a desire to match her own. "No one would dare stay away tonight. One does hope to see some scandal. Perhaps Lady Elizabeth will ride a horse across the ballroom to show her disregard for us all."

He regarded her coldly. "Is that truly what has brought them here? The hope of seeing their hosts disgraced?"

She shrugged. "One has to amuse oneself somehow, does one not?"

And indeed, she reflected as she whirled about, she was amusing herself mightily tonight. All of her plans were working out well. Lady Elizabeth had fallen from grace, and it had not even taken Ariadne's artful hand to accomplish it.

The viscount had tumbled top over tail in love with her, and would soon be ripe for the plucking. In the interim, she planned to satisfy herself and revenge herself at the same time.

"You are certainly looking well tonight," Lord Meridan told

her. "A splendid gown, and no more of it than one would wish."

Ariadne laughed lightly and fluttered her eyelashes. "I am so glad you came, my lord. Otherwise all this effort would have been wasted."

He nodded in recognition of the compliment and clasped her even more firmly as they danced.

The marquis apparently had noticed no change in her attitude toward him, and seemed if anything more attached to her than before, she decided, watching him surreptitiously. No doubt he thought she was being loyal in the face of his reversals, and she intended to let him think that.

Ariadne had no intention of consigning herself to a life with the awkward young viscount without one more fling in the bed of the handsomest man of her acquaintance. And what a comeuppance it would be for him, to take her back into his arms, only to discover that she had used him one last time. It was no more than he deserved for trying to keep her ignorant of his poverty while he secured her fortune as well as her person for himself!

She was hard put not to grin broadly as she noticed Lady Elizabeth standing on the sidelines, her heart in her eyes as she gazed at the marquis. Yes, things were going very well for Ariadne Singleton that night.

The same could not be said of Hester. She had never in her life imagined that her come-out would be such a disaster. The worst of it was the underhandedness, the duplicity of their guests. If they had not come at all, at least she could have nursed her wounds in private! But no, everyone must watch her, and she must pretend not to notice the lack of interest of her dancing partners and the coolness of her own reception in contrast to the enthusiasm the young bucks showed for Alicia and the other young beauties.

The worst of it all was Sir Percy. He, of course, took no pleasure in their downfall, but he seemed content to dance only once with her. He was spending most of the evening in the card room with his gentlemen friends, as if the success of her debut were of no special interest to him.

Hester blinked back a tear and put on a somewhat uncertain smile as she curtseyed to an aging dandy and accepted his arm for the gavotte.

She kept her head high as the dance began, aware that everyone would notice any betrayal of emotion. So this was how Lizzie had felt at her own come-out, when she had seen that she was not a success. For the first time, Hester found herself in sympathy with her sister. She had never before given a moment's thought to how difficult it must have been this past year, to carry oneself off gracefully despite one's social failure. At least she, Hester, had the consolation that her situation did not stem from her own person, and therefore might someday be forgotten, at least by others.

But Lizzie had failed because she was not the sort of brittle, beautiful girl whom society prized, and never would be. For one unaccustomed moment, Hester felt herself in her sister's shoes. No wonder Lizzie had tried all those stratagems! And, in the end, it seemed one was at the mercy of these heartless strangers no matter what one did. Perhaps Mary had had the right idea all along.

As she turned in the dance, her notice fell on Alicia Tonquin. Oddly enough, the girl had looked dissatisfied all evening, despite her own warm reception, and now frowned mightily as she walked out onto the dance floor with the Viscount Winston. She ought to flirt with him more, or she would lose him entirely, Hester reflected.

However, Alicia was not feeling in a particularly flirtatious mood at the moment. Indeed, she was feeling mightily put out. The viscount had paid her scant heed so far, and from his demeanour appeared to have requested a set only from a sense of obligation due to his longtime friendship with the Tonquins.

"You are, um, looking very well tonight, Alicia," the viscount stammered as the new set began, his gaze almost at once transferring itself to the voluptuous form of Ariadne Singleton, halfway across the dance floor.

"How kind of you to notice," she answered. "Especially when you have hardly looked at me at all."

"Beg pardon?" He gaped at her as they moved through the gavotte.

"You have been staring at Mrs. Singleton all evening!" Alicia declared. "I did not realise she was ill."

"Ill?" He frowned. "Is she? I hope it is nothing serious."

Alicia glared at him. "Do you mean to tell me you have fixed upon a woman who has not even the attraction of some serious disease?''

He shook his head in puzzlement. ''I fear I do not follow you.''

''You are making a cake of yourself, John!'' she burst out. ''Mooning after that woman! Can't you see what she is? She's years older than you and the only thing about you that interests her is that you stand to inherit a dukedom!''

She bit her lip. Never had she intended to speak so forthrightly or so rudely, and she was taken aback to see the colour drain from his cheeks. ''Oh, John, I'm sorry,'' she whispered. ''I didn't mean to offend you.''

''I assure you, you've done nothing of the kind.'' He looked at her as if she were a complete stranger. ''Indeed, I'm deeply grateful to you, Miss Tonquin, for showing me your true nature.''

''John!'' She stared at him, searching desperately for some way to pierce his coldness. Finally she forced herself to utter the painful words: ''If you must know, I'm jealous.''

''Oh?'' His look softened not one whit. ''Perhaps you are jealous, but not as you would have me believe. I think you attribute to Mrs. Singleton your own motives, Miss Tonquin. It is my title that has drawn you, is it not? And you cannot conceive that another woman should see in me anything beyond that, but I assure you, in Ariadne's case, you are entirely wrong.''

Ariadne. So he called her by her first name. What intimacies had already taken place between them? Alicia stared at him hopelessly as the dance ended. ''Someday you'll find out who really cares for you!'' she blurted, then turned and fled.

Beth caught her just before she would have stumbled into a large potted fern. ''I'm sorry to see you so distressed, Alicia,'' she said. ''This ball is a disaster for everyone, it seems. Shall I find your mother?''

Alicia shook her head, fighting back the tears. ''No, Lizzie. Oh, I'm afraid you warned us too late. She's already snared him. He can see no evil in her, and all I've done is to turn him against me!''

Beth sighed. ''I shan't try to give you any more advice,'' she said. ''My life is too tangled for me to dare bestow my counsel on anyone else. But there is one consolation.''

"What's that?" Alicia asked.

"Mrs. Singleton appears to have won both our gentlemen friends," Beth told her. "It is unlawful in England to take two husbands, so either she will have to move to some heathen land or one of them will be rejected."

"He thinks so little of me, it would do me no good," Alicia said. "Thank you for trying to cheer me, though, Lizzie. And I shan't think of him any longer. After all, this is *my* season and there are plenty of other men in the world."

Beth managed a smile as one of Alicia's young admirers approached and secured the dark-haired young beauty for the next dance. Broken hearts do mend, she told herself. Except, perhaps, Louis Chumley's.

That thought returned her to the dismals, and the resumption of the orchestra pounded through her head. Unable to bear the noise any longer, Beth slipped away.

Once outside the crowded ballroom, she began to feel better, and made her way slowly through a corridor to her favourite room in the house.

It was the glass-roofed, plant-filled orangerie, where Lady Fairchild indulged her passion for roses while in the city. In addition to the bright pink flowers, the room sported the rich green-leafed shapes of orange and lemon trees, kept to a manageable size by being root-bound in large pots.

Beth sank onto a bench and inhaled the fresh, sweet smell of lemon blossoms. She could almost imagine herself at that moment in some biblical setting, in a garden of some exotic land.

A whisper of tobacco smoke told her she was not alone. "Who's there?" Beth called, startled.

One of the small trees rustled, and the marquis stepped into view, carefully extinguishing his cigar in a receptacle. For a moment, words deserted Beth.

The diffuse moonlight and distant flicker of tapers lent a sense of mystery to his tall, erect figure, emphasizing the shadowy hollows of his cheeks and throat and the bright depth of his eyes. He could almost have been some exotic sheik, come to remove her to a make-believe world.

He stared at her for a moment before commenting. "Tired of dancing so soon, Lady Beth?"

She closed her eyes, breathing in the scent of lemon blossoms. "I had rather be here," she said, looking up at him. "Or in the country, or almost anywhere but London. It does not suit me."

"Especially not tonight?" He stood regarding her expressionlessly, and Beth felt her blood quicken at his nearness. It took all her self-discipline to remind herself that she was responsible for the death of one of this man's friends, and that no amount of moonlight and lemon flowers would ever smooth the gap between them.

"Why especially not tonight?" she challenged.

He shrugged. "That business with Brummell. Rather unfair it should reflect on you, I suppose, but perhaps not."

"Pray continue."

"You scheme well." The marquis nodded to her, as if in deference to her talents. "You could not have known the Beau would be so indiscreet as to insult the prince directly."

"I see." Beth folded her hands in her lap, determined not to retreat before his insinuations. "In your view then I cultivated Brummell to gain myself a high position in society, and so to you it is merely a matter of amusement that all these carefully woven plans should go awry."

For one instant something like hurt flickered in his eyes. "I do not take pleasure in . . ." He caught himself and turned away, his face hidden by the shadows as he continued. "I do not stoop to amuse myself with these matters, Lady Beth. But there is a certain justice here. You have pushed yourself forward with little regard for the feelings of others, and now you receive the same treatment yourself."

A prickling in her eyes warned Beth that her composure was threatened, but she caught her hands tightly together and forced herself to reply calmly. "I know you refer to the matter of Mr Chumley, and I regret that my memory has not yet returned. Therefore I cannot defend myself; I cannot even chastise myself for I do not know if I deserve it."

"Surely what is common knowledge . . ."

"Oh?" She met his gaze directly. "Am I then to judge the truth by what others tell me?"

"It ill becomes anyone, man or woman, to run from the facts, however unpleasant." He searched her face for something, almost longingly.

"A strange sentiment, coming from you," she said. "Sir Percy tells me you plan to retreat to Cornwall."

"Retreat is not precisely the term I would put on it," he said, appearing surprised at this turn of the conversation.

"Well, I would," said Beth. "I beg your pardon for speaking of a matter that is none of my concern, but if you have suffered financial difficulties, that is no reason to shut yourself away as if you were in disgrace. Gambling losses would be one thing, but as I well know, one cannot stop a ship from sinking or resurrect one that has gone down, however much one might wish to."

He leaned against a pillar, regarding her with some interest. "What would you have me do then, Lady Beth? Go about as if nothing had changed, and spend my way into debt?"

"Not at all," she said. "You would have to live with more circumspection, perhaps, but that cannot concern your true friends."

"One's false friends can be quite cruel, as you have reason to know," he observed.

"If I, a mere girl, can face up to them, I hardly think a man of your stature would flee with his tail between his legs," she said, and was pleased to see annoyance written across his face. Perhaps he would reconsider after all; for even if she could not have him, Beth did not like to see the marquis turn himself into an outcast.

"My decisions have nothing to do with cowardice," he snapped. "It is merely that I do not relish receiving pity."

"No one but a fool would ever pity you," she said. "You are quite an imposing figure, Lord Meridan. I am sure that even penniless you should find a way to make something of your life. I do not see how anyone could think . . ." She caught herself midsentence.

"Think what, pray tell?" As he coiled onto the bench beside her, Beth found it difficult to keep her thoughts straight.

"Oh . . . that you might find a way out of your difficulties by marrying well," she said.

"And who has said that?"

"No one in particular." Her answer came too quickly, and her nervousness did not escape him.

"I thought you were devoted to telling the truth, Lady Beth," he said. "You disappoint me."

Beth sighed. "You will think I am inventing tales, but very well, I shall tell you. When Mrs. Singleton learned of your predicament, that was her first reaction, that you had sought to win her for her fortune. But I can see she has thought better of it since then."

He brooded thoughtfully for a moment. Had he noticed Ariadne's increased attentions to the viscount? Beth wondered. But surely Mrs. Singleton would have broken off with the marquis if she were angry with him.

"You are a cunning minx," Lord Meridan said at last. "You almost persuaded me to believe you. Perhaps it is your intention to remind me that you as well stand to inherit a considerable sum. Or perhaps you merely wish to deny Ariadne what you yourself cannot have."

Beth glared at him. "I don't know why I waste my breath talking with you! You twist everything I say! Why should I care what passes between you and Mrs. Singleton, or whether you run off to Cornwall? Suit yourself, my lord."

"I intend to." Before she knew it, he had grasped her tightly about the waist and pulled her against his shoulder, throwing her off-balance. As she opened her mouth to protest, he bent and claimed her with a deep, probing kiss.

Against her will, she found herself responding, her body warming to his caresses. He leaned over and traced her throat with his lips as his hands stroked upward from her waist. She felt the heat of his breath just above her bodice, on the soft swell of her breasts.

"Lord Meridan!" Shocked by his boldness and her own response, she somehow found the strength to pull away and come to her feet. "Whatever can you be thinking?"

Breathing hard, he sat where he was, his eyes locked into hers. "What I am thinking, my dear Lady Beth, is that an honest woman like Ariadne Singleton does not scruple to share herself with a man she admires. Whereas you wish only to spear the fish and cast him aside, and not even let him enjoy the bait. No wonder Chumley was driven to distraction. But I am not such a fool."

Without waiting for her reaction, he strode out of the room. Distantly, Beth realised the orchestra was still playing in the ballroom. Her absence would soon be noticed and remarked upon, but she no longer cared.

Torn by her own unexpected response to the marquis and wounded deeply by his rejection, she fled in tears to the sanctuary of her room.

=11=

THE MARQUIS'S DISAPPEARANCE at the same time as Lady Elizabeth's had not gone unremarked by Mrs. Singleton, even as she continued chatting gaily with the Viscount Winston. Nor did she fail to notice that Lord Meridan reappeared looking distracted, and that Beth did not turn up again all evening.

What had passed between them? The marquis continued his attentions, and Ariadne might almost have thought she was mistaken in her conclusion that a conversation had taken place. But no, there was a subtle difference in the marquis's attitude, a shade of distance that had not been there before. A seed of suspicion had been planted, and she must destroy it before it grew.

"Perhaps I should call on Lady Elizabeth privately," she murmured as Lord Meridan swept her through a waltz, the superfine of his coat feeling silky beneath her hand.

"Why should you wish to do such a thing?" he inquired.

"To give her a bit of friendly advice," said Ariadne with a calculated semblance of artlessness. "Being such a rough-and-tumble sort, perhaps she does not realise how best to deal with scandal."

"And how is that?" asked his lordship.

Ariadne smiled as they turned and moved rapidly in time with the music. "Why, by creating another scandal of course," she said. "I would advise her to spread some tattle about another lady— someone she does not like, of course, someone she considers deserving of it. Naturally, she should tell only what is true, although some less scrupulous persons might actually invent their on-dits."

From the marquis's frown, she gathered that she had hit the mark. So that wretched little Elizabeth had dared to tell him that Ariadne knew him to be a fortune hunter! Well, she had not got away with it.

The marquis continued his attentions, clear proof that Beth's plot had failed.

He reluctantly surrendered Ariadne at last to the viscount, to whom she had promised the supper dance, and she went in on John's arm to dine. Happily, the Fairchilds had scattered small tables about the supper room and the veranda, and with only a small amount of manoeuvering, Ariadne was able to arrange to be quite alone with the young man.

He heaped their plates with lobster patties and trout Provencale, roast swan with sweet sauce, green beans, salad, and a French banana cream. Ariadne picked delicately at her food, although it was much to her taste. One did not wish to seem gluttonous.

As was his wont, the viscount stammered when he spoke, struggling to make conversation in the most awkward matter. Once they were married, Ariadne would dare to rebuke him for this annoying habit, but now she pretended to listen attentively and added gay bits of gossip to keep things moving.

From where they sat on the veranda, she could see that wench Alicia Tonquin eyeing her resentfully. No doubt the chit was already scheming to draw the viscount away and, to be sure, Ariadne had to remind herself that he had once admired Beth Fairchild and then lost interest. There was a distinct possibility he would prove equally as fickle with her.

She must lead him to offer for her quickly. Yet from the gentleman's social ineptness, it was clear that left to his own devices he might take a year or more to work up the nerve.

Manipulating men was Ariadne's special talent, and she did not intend to be found lacking now. As soon as her companion ran out of words and sat in uncomfortable silence, she heaved a large sigh.

"Whatever . . . whatever is the matter?" he asked anxiously. "Is it too cold for you here, Ariadne? Shall we go indoors?"

She suppressed an expression of irritation. "Not at all, my dear John," she whispered. "I yearn to have you to myself for as long as possible this evening."

His brow creased as he contemplated the many potential shadings of this statement. "You're not going away somewhere? I—I'm not sure what you mean."

Again, Ariadne sighed deeply, aware that the movement revealed an extra expanse of bosom. The viscount's eyes seemed almost to bulge from his face.

"Not going away, precisely," she said. "But you see . . . ah, how can I put this? You are so young. To you, life is only beginning."

"You are youth itself," he protested, sounding a bit ridiculous mouthing the poetic phrase he had most likely gleaned from some journal. "You are all that is lovely and desirable. Er . . . pray continue, Ariadne."

She gazed deep into his eyes, noting how watery and colourless they appeared in the moonlight. "A woman in my position finds herself at the mercy of society. True, I am wealthy, but I am still too young and . . . well, some gentlemen are kind enough to call me beautiful. This situation arouses jealousy and gossip."

"I know precisely what you mean!" His forceful words caught her off guard.

"You do?" she ventured.

"Alicia Tonquin only this very evening tried to have me believe that you were solely interested in my prospects," he declared, with more spirit than he had ever exhibited before. "I am sure her motive can only have been jealousy."

"Of course." Ariadne's mind was working rapidly. So the moon-faced Miss Tonquin had shown her claws. Or had she been prompted? She recalled seeing the girl conversing intimately with Lady Elizabeth earlier that evening. A dangerous minx, that one, but not near clever enough. "So you can understand why I might find myself . . . not entirely free to live as I might choose," she went on.

"I'm afraid I don't . . . don't understand, entirely," said Lord Winston, leaning forward and peering at her with puppylike devotion.

Ariadne considered heaving yet another sigh but thought the better of it. "In short, I have received a proposal of marriage from an elderly gentleman. Not the sort who might engage my heart, of course, but he offers his services as my protector. I fear that if things go on the way they are, soon some scandal will attach itself to my name—through malicious gossip, of course—and I will find myself shunned and set aside.''

"But you cannot . . ." So distraught was the viscount that he could not complete his sentence, and even in the dim light his face appeared flushed. "Surely, Ariadne, you cannot contemplate becoming leg-shackled to some old . . . some old goat!''

She gazed soulfully into the distance. "A woman is not free in this world of ours, dear, dear John. She cannot always do as she pleases.''

"But you do not love him?" he pleaded.

"No, indeed not," she said. "Nor could I ever feel for him the sentiments I harbour for you . . . oh, but please forgive me, I speak out of turn.''

"Not at all," he declared, and Ariadne saw that the lamb had been skilfully led to the slaughter. "I do assure you, my feelings for you are of the tenderest nature. I cannot abide. . . . Well! Here is an idea! What a chump I am not to have thought of it before!''

The sigh Ariadne uttered this time was quite real. The fellow was as slow as an old carthorse! Would he never come to the point?

"You must marry me instead!" said the viscount. "That is, if you will have me. I should get down on my knees for this, should I not?''

"No, no!" she objected quickly. It was far too soon for the marquis to learn of her betrothal, and he would surely learn of it quickly were John seen on his knees before her. "I assure you, under the circumstances it is not necessary. But John, have you thought out this matter carefully? Already you have been told lies about me. Are you prepared to face the world, with a wife two or three years older than you"—although seven or eight was more like it—"and of far greater experience? I beg you not to leap hastily into so serious an arrangement.''

"My mind is made up!" He sat back and beamed at her. "I love you, Ariadne, and I cannot wait to make you mine! Will you have me?''

"I should be delighted." She lowered her eyes demurely. "You do me a great honour, sir.''

He clasped her hand and raised it to his lips, kissing it ardently and somewhat damply. "Pray notify the newspapers at once, and we shall set a date as soon as all matters may be arranged."

Ariadne carefully extracted her hand and leaned her chin on it. "But it may be weeks, even months, before your family can attend, and then there are the gowns and the flowers. I think you are a man of action, John Winston, and cannot bear such delay."

"Indeed, you are right," he said, glowing with pleasure at her flattery. "But what choice is there?"

Leaning forward, she said in a low, intimate tone, "There is Gretna Green, dearest."

"An elopement?" He hesitated, but only for a moment. "It would come as something of a shock to Mama and Papa, perhaps, but I think you are right, sweetest love. Shall we leave at once—tonight, perhaps? It is not past midnight."

Briefly, Ariadne was tempted to agree, but just then she heard the marquis's voice some distance away as he conversed with an unseen partner. She wanted him again, wanted to rouse him to great passion and then laugh in his face as she spurned him and went to her younger, wealthier, and higher-born suitor. The man had plotted to make a fool of her—worse, to take her money as well as her body—and he would not be so easily set free.

"It is only a matter of a week until I give my masked ball," she said. "Think what sport that would be—to disappear from my own party, and turn up the next day married! Don't you think that would be famous, John? We should be the envy of all London. How romantic it would be. Shall we do it?"

"Oh, yes!" John exclaimed so loudly that he surely could be heard at other tables. "What a clever idea!"

The details were left for another day, and Ariadne sailed back into the ballroom on her fiance's arm, luxuriating in the envious glare of Alicia Tonquin.

The sound of the music wove its way through Beth's troubled dreams until the early morning hours. Her lips burned where the marquis had kissed them, the memory filling her with shame and confusion.

Surely he had meant to insult her, she thought, during her wakeful moments. How amused he must have been when she responded like some wanton!

In the morning, puffy-eyed and down at heart, she was forced to endure her mother's grim fury at their late breakfast.

"Now, William," Lady Fairchild addressed her husband, "you see what comes of allowing Elizabeth to gallivant about London? She has destroyed Hester's chances for the season, as well as her own. Shall we not send her away before she does any more damage?"

His lordship lowered his morning newspaper with a great show of annoyance. "And what would be the purpose of that?" he grumbled. "We should have to send our carriage to the country for several days to take her, and how should we get about then?"

The lady of the house drummed her fingers on the table. Hester had not come down yet, and Beth, reluctant to engage in an open quarrel with her mother, sipped wearily at her third cup of coffee.

"I am sure we can make do with the chaise," said Lady Fairchild.

"Yes, and what of a husband?" harrumphed Lord Fairchild. "They don't grow them in the fields, you know."

"No one will call on her here!" Lady Fairchild's voice rose with a quaver of semi-hysteria. "No gentleman will ever again come to visit Elizabeth here in London!"

The butler entered after a polite knock and said, with such perfect timing that Beth wondered if he had not been lingering outside the door, "Sir Percy Stem has come to take Lady Elizabeth for a drive. Shall I say she is not at home?"

"There, you see?" Lord Fairchild returned triumphantly to his newspaper.

So it was that Beth, who fortunately had worn a new morning gown of pale russet silk in an attempt to revive her spirits, found herself riding out with Sir Percy in a phaeton he had borrowed from Lord Meridan, his own having broken a wheel.

He noticed her pallor at once. "Is something wrong, Lady Beth?" He guided the horses carefully around a wagon loaded with potatoes. "I noticed that you retired early last night. The evening must have been difficult for you."

She contemplated briefly telling him of her troubles with Lord

Meridan, but she dared not take even him that much into her confidence. "Yes, I found it extremely trying," she said. "Let us not talk about it. In fact, there is a different subject I wish to discuss with you."

As they dodged around yet another wagon, she added, "Could we not find some place more peaceful to carry on this conversation?"

Not having done more than nibble at her devilled kidneys and eggs that morning, she readily accepted his suggestion that they continue their talk over hot chocolate and biscuits in Bond Street.

The chocolate shop was nearly filled, but they found a table by the window. Once they had given their orders, Beth looked straight into Sir Percy's hazel eyes and said, "Tell me why you have come calling on me this morning, now that Hester is out."

"I beg your pardon?" His look of surprise was tempered by a teasing smile. "Out of what?"

"Out of patience, no doubt." She shook her head in amazement. "Surely you do not think me fool enough to believe that you are enamoured of me? I had believed you came so that you could see Hester, since she was not yet out, but now I admit to being puzzled."

Sir Percy rested his chin on the heel of his hand. "Must I explain everything?"

Beth shrugged. "Not if you don't wish, but I am not taken in. I suppose I should thank you. My parents were on the point of exiling me to the country when you came to call. Your visit persuaded my father that his cause of finding me a husband in London is not yet lost."

"Always happy to be of service," declared Sir Percy as the waiter arrived with their chocolate.

Outside, Ariadne Singleton happened at the moment to be passing in her carriage. Although she did not customarily arise until noon, she had a fitting that morning for her costume for the ball.

Espying the marquis's phaeton, she found her attention drawn by a figure in the window—that of Elizabeth Fairchild. Beside her lounged a gentleman whose face was turned away, but there could be no doubt who it must be.

Angrily, Ariadne considered what action she might take now.

She had seen the danger the previous season. His lordship, while disapproving of the young lady's antics, had been much taken with her. It was only good luck that Louis Chumley had confided in Ariadne before he left for America, telling her that he had run up such debts as to be in imminent danger of imprisonment.

His last hope had been to marry an heiress, but Lord Fairchild had dismissed his offer. On the eve of his departure, not wishing his true state of finances to be known even by his friends at the club, Louis had put it about that he was departing because of a broken heart.

After his untimely death, it had taken only a little embellishment on Ariadne's part to work up a credible tale that the young man had been misled and much abused by Lady Elizabeth. A few words in the right ears and the tale was spread, dovetailing neatly with what Chumley himself had told his friends.

Now perhaps she might embroider the story a bit more. Elizabeth must not triumph, and the marquis must not find happiness, not if Ariadne had anything to do with it.

But the idea that came to mind now was a dangerous one. It would force Ariadne to reveal more of her private relationship with Louis than she wished, to explain how she came by her information. And she did not wish all London to know that she and the young man had once been lovers, and that that was why he continued to confide in her until his departure. No, it was not worth so great a risk, not with her elopement and a dukedom at stake. But Lady Elizabeth had best not provoke her too far.

"I wish you would tell me why you continue to call on me," Beth was saying to Sir Percy, unaware of Mrs. Singleton's carriage passing by outside. "Society is so full of intrigues, and I have so little talent for it."

"Do you know, it is an unfortunate thing that you and I have not fallen in love," said Sir Percy, fingering a biscuit. "I do admire you, Lady Beth. Whereas Hester is childish and selfish, quite maddening altogether."

"As I thought," observed Beth. "You are in love with her."

He peered over the rim of his chocolate cup. "Hopelessly. And she has no interest in a poor bloke like me."

Beth considered. "She had high hopes of making her mark in society, but I fear I have dashed them. She might settle for you after all, you know."

He shook his head. "I do not want a reluctant wife. I want her as mad for me as I am for her."

His response drew a smile. "Perhaps she is fonder of you than you think," Beth said. "Of course, then you will have the obstacle of my father, who is not enamoured of impoverished young men."

"I shall deal with him when the time comes," Sir Percy said with quiet confidence.

"You know, I should be angry with you." Beth reflected before she went on. "You are toying with my affections for the purpose of making my sister jealous. What a cruel man you are!"

"Nonsense," said Sir Percy. "Do you think me too blind to notice that your affections are engaged elsewhere?"

She blushed. "Am I so obvious?"

"To a friend, yes."

"And the . . . object of my affections?" she pushed on. "What of his sentiments?"

It was Sir Percy's turn to think for a moment before speaking. "He is more difficult to read. A proud man, as you know. Loyal to his friends, especially dead ones. Although I have always had a hard time of it to believe that tale about you."

"The marquis will never forgive me, then," she said dully. "It is as I feared."

"I never thought I'd say it, but Brett is a crashing fool," said Sir Percy. "Anyone can see the two of you would suit perfectly, and if it weren't for this business of your missing memory, I suspect you'd have the misunderstanding cleared up by now."

"If it is a misunderstanding," Beth reminded him.

The crowd had increased, and they saw that others were waiting for their table. The two departed, enjoying a leisurely ride home.

Sir Percy is right, thought Beth. If only we could fall in love with each other, how easy things would be.

Then she remembered Lord Meridan's embrace the previous evening, and the fire he had aroused within her. She would never love another man like that, not if she lived to be a hundred.

When they arrived home, Sir Percy lingered for a moment in the entrance hall, conversing rather loudly. Beth knew he was hoping for a glimpse of Hester, nor was he disappointed.

The young lady herself entered the hallway within moments, clad in a rose silk dress that revealed a bit more of her throat than usual. Hester managed to look surprised at seeing their guest.

"I did not mean to disturb you," she said quickly.

"Not at all." Sir Percy bowed. "You look lovely this morning. Now that you are out, I have no doubt that you will continue to blossom until you are indeed a rival to your sister."

Here he favoured Beth with a melting look, and she was hard put not to burst into laughter.

"A rival to my sister, is it?" demanded Hester, advancing with hands on hips. "I certainly have no intention of vying with her for your affections, sir, as you should well know by now!"

"Oh, I do beg your pardon, I fear I have not made myself clear," said Sir Percy. "I meant only to compliment you both."

But Hester would not be pacified. "I suppose you think I would actually enjoy being called upon by you at any hour of the morning, and dragged out to ride in a borrowed phaeton—don't think I haven't noticed!"

So she had been watching them out the window, thought Beth.

"I must apologise to Lady Beth for not having my own repaired yet," said Sir Percy. "The wheelwright tells me the streets are in such a shocking state, that he cannot keep up with his business."

"Oh, certainly!" Hester flared. "I am sure your previous unpaid bills with him—for I have no doubt there are several—have no bearing on the matter."

"Hester!" Beth stared, shocked, at her younger sister, who had never before ventured in public this far from her meek facade. "You are insulting my guest!"

Sir Percy's amusement had vanished, and Beth sensed a strain in his voice as he addressed her. "I can see that the manner of my transport and my financial state are distressing to Lady Hester. I certainly would not wish to burden her further with my presence. Good day, my dearest Lady Beth."

He bent over her hand, and then strode out the door without a backward glance.

Hester stared after him, her face a study in conflicting emotions.

"Did you mean that?" Beth asked.

"Did I mean what?" Hester eyed her suspiciously.

"That you should not wish him to call upon you, because he is poor and cannot afford to have his own carriage fixed?" she said.

Hester looked down at the marble floor. "I don't know, Beth. Oh, what is the use, anyway? It isn't me he wants, it's you!" And she fled from the hall.

== 12 ==

MRS. SINGLETON HAD been almost two months in London without calling upon Lady Smythe, and it was not lost upon her that duty required a visit to thank her hostess for the houseparty in the country.

However, Ariadne might still have come up with sufficient excuses to keep her distance had she not been aware that Lady Smythe was the most dedicated gossip in London. It would not do for her to bear rancour against Ariadne. John was not a duke yet, and the cutting edge of her tongue could do the couple great harm once their union became known and a topic of discussion.

For although John was as moon-eyed as ever about their elopement the following night, Ariadne knew quite well that his family would disapprove. Her own birth was certainly not impeccable, nor was her reputation. And they had no need of her wealth.

So she forced herself, one morning in early May, to call upon Lady Smythe.

Her hostess, gowned in unbecoming pink gabardine with a matching turban, received her in the morning room with politeness but no warmth.

"I fear I have been remiss," said Ariadne as she accepted a cup of tea. "I wished to call upon you sooner, Lady Smythe."

"So one would think," sniffed the older lady. "Will you have a strawberry tart?"

Ariadne smiled and shook her head. Once she was wed, there would be plenty of time to indulge in such fattening delicacies, but for now she must still guard her figure carefully.

"I believe we may have the honour of your presence at my

masked ball tomorrow night?" Ariadne continued. "I do so hope you will enjoy it."

Her hostess seemed to thaw slightly. "Well, if you must know, I have the most wonderful costume—would you believe my husband absolutely insisted? I fear it was frightfully expensive."

"How fortunate you are to have such a husband," Ariadne murmured, wondering how the rotund and awkward woman across from her had ever found a match. The dark woods of the room and the heavy gold velvet curtains at the window showed a want of lightness and spirit that pervaded the entire house. Yet clearly Lord Smythe loved both his lumpy wife and his lumpy house.

"Oh, I assure you, he is usually not so generous," Lady Smythe giggled girlishly. "But his ventures have done amazingly well this year, thanks to Lord Meridan's advice."

"Beg pardon?"

"Brett Meridan. He suggested that Lord Smythe invest in some of the same ships as he, and a splendid suggestion it was," said Lady Smythe, quite insensible of the tempest she was arousing in her visitor's breast.

"This comes as something of a surprise," Ariadne said carefully, setting down her cup. "I was informed that he had suffered financial reverses this year."

"Oh, my dear, whoever can have told you that?" Lady Smythe shook her head. "The way some people will gossip! And without the least regard for truth! No, I assure you, my dear, Lord Meridan is wealthier this year than ever he was."

Ariadne was trying with difficulty to digest this new information and what it might mean. Still, she found it hard to believe. "Could he not have succeeded in those projects he shared with your husband, yet had far more serious setbacks in other ones?"

An expression of annoyance crossed Lady Smythe's florid face. "Do you not think I would have heard of it, I who have friends in every corner?" she demanded. "I assure you, only this week he purchased a fine team of chestnuts at Tattersall's, and they do not come cheap, believe me."

Ariadne knew quite well that a man down on his luck could not afford horses from the best stables in London, nor was the marquis the sort to run up bills he could not pay.

Somehow she managed to stumble through the next few minutes' conversation as she tried to make sense of her jumbled thoughts.

One thing was clear to her. She had been tricked. And by none other than Elizabeth Fairchild. She had underestimated the wench, and had believed every lying word about the marquis. So all Lady Beth's proclamations of honesty came down to this: She had thrown Ariadne Singleton, the best schemer of them all, so far off the scent that she had almost lost the marquis.

Almost, but not quite. Ariadne breathed a silent sigh of thanks to the desire for revenge that had made her hide her true sentiments. As far as the marquis knew, Ariadne's attitude toward him had not changed.

But there was the awkward matter of the elopement to be got out of. And Ariadne could not forget that Elizabeth had had several weeks to pursue the marquis without fear of serious competition.

It was an easy matter, then, to steer the conversation with Lady Smythe to the Fairchilds—a mention of Brummell's continuing disgrace, then a discussion of the Fairchilds' ball—and Ariadne had a clear field.

"It is really too bad about Lady Beth," she said. "She has ruined her chances, I fear."

"Difficult girl," snorted Lady Smythe. "Ragmannered, if you ask me."

That was a good sign. It would have been far more difficult to have persuaded someone who looked favourably on the young lady in question, thought Ariadne.

"I would not be too harsh upon her," she said. "I made mistakes in my youth, also."

"Who didn't?" agreed her hostess. "But this insolence of hers . . . and then there was that shocking business of Louis Chumley. Of course, I never actually saw her behave improperly toward him, but I understand she led him quite a merry chase. Heartless chit!"

"Indeed." Ariadne had to force herself to repress a smile. "Well, one cannot bring back the dead. But I must say I am shocked that . . . well, that's neither here nor there. She's no prospects for a husband this year, nor should she have."

"Oh, but you're wrong." Lady Smythe leaned forward confidingly. "They do say Sir Percy Stem has been to call on her more than once."

"I never thought Sir Percy to be such a fortune hunter," said Ariadne.

Her hostess looked puzzled. "It must be owned she is not unattractive. He could have more motive than merely her portion."

"Yes, but surely he knows . . ." Ariadne paused just long enough for the older woman to prompt her.

"Well? Do go on. Knows what?"

"About her and . . ." Ariadne stared modestly down at her hands. "Perhaps I should say no more."

"Of course you must!" cried the very frustrated lady. "About her and whom? Her and Chumley? I am sure he knows that!"

Ariadne contemplated the merits of heaving a sigh but decided it might strike even Lady Smythe as too dramatic. "She . . . may I confide in you?"

It was a question calculated to stir sympathy in the hardest-hearted gossip. "Confide in me? My dear, you need have no fear that your words will ever leave this room!"

As if reassured, Ariadne continued. "Chumley and I were old acquaintances. It was in me he confided before departing for America. . . ." Here she paused to dab at her eyes with a kerchief.

She found herself regarded with a sceptical eye. "Why should he have confided in you?"

"We had . . . at one time . . . oh, Lady Smythe, this is most difficult," Ariadne breathed. "At one point, after my bereavement, Louis Chumley and I were intimate. Even afterward, he continued to feel that I was the only one in whom he could confide. Oh, I beg your forgiveness if I have offended you."

Lady Smythe was far from being offended. "Nonsense. Anyone can understand that a widow might, er, be tempted to stray. It is not such a shocking thing. But what of Lady Elizabeth?"

"Before he departed," said Ariadne, "he told me that on one occasion—in the garden, I believe it was—she had allowed him to become intimate with her as well."

Her words fell into a pool of silence. She looked up to see her hostess staring at her in disbelief and delight. "In the garden?" gasped Lady Smythe in a choked voice. "Are you quite sure, my dear Ariadne?"

"Oh, yes," she said. "It was this that naturally led him to believe she intended to be his wife."

"I should think so!"

"Then he was refused. I suppose she thought he would not be believed if he spread such a tale, and indeed, he was far too honourable to do so."

"Indeed," said Lady Smythe, her distracted air indicating that her thoughts were already running ahead to all the implications of this revelation.

"Naturally one would expect her to withdraw from society," Ariadne went on. "At the very least, she would be honour-bound to warn any serious suitor that he was in the way of receiving damaged goods. But apparently it is her intention to continue her shockingly disreputable behaviour, her disregard for customs and consideration."

"How well I know her feelings on that score!" agreed the older lady. "It is just the sort of thing she would do."

"But naturally, no one else must hear of this," Ariadne cautioned. "It was not Chumley's wish to spread it about, nor is it mine. I mean her no harm, you understand, Lady Smythe."

"Of course, of course," said her hostess. "No one shall hear of this, I assure you."

A few minutes later, Ariadne excused herself and went on her way well satisfied.

Half of London would have heard the tale by the next evening, and whether Beth attended the costume ball or not, there would be a delicious scandal.

The consequences would be immediate. The girl would be banished from polite society, and off limits as a potential wife for any respectable man. Meridan, already convinced that she had wronged Chumley, would be doubly outraged to learn how far she had gone with him. And any tender spark he might have nurtured in his breast would be extinguished forever.

You should not play at games unless you are prepared to play them to the hilt, Mrs. Singleton reminded herself as she was handed into her carriage. It was too bad Lady Elizabeth had not learned that lesson. For now she had played and lost.

As Ariadne anticipated, the rumour was not long in leaving Lady Smythe's lips. That good lady, in fact, could scarcely wait to go calling. By late afternoon, three friends had been acquainted with the story. By evening, each of them had told a number of others.

The account reached Lady Fairchild's ears the next morning as she attended a fitting. Overhearing it accidentally, she emerged and demanded to know the full story, and was, with some embarrassment, rapidly enlightened.

Lord Fairchild was out on business, but directly he returned in midafternoon his wife imparted the information to him, and Beth found herself summoned to his study.

She did not often enter the booklined chamber, with its reclusive smell of old wood and leather, and the moment she saw her father's face she knew something dreadful had occurred.

"What is it, father?" she asked.

The Viscount Fairchild regarded her irritably, as infuriated by having to endure this confrontation as by the offense itself.

"Your mother tells me there is a story in wide circulation concerning you," he began.

Beth took a deep breath. "What is it this time?"

He scowled. "Don't take that tone with me, young lady! It is said that you compromised yourself with Louis Chumley."

She gazed at him in perplexity. "Do you mean that old tale, that I led him on and then broke his heart?"

"Compromised is compromised!" he boomed. "We are speaking here of your ruin, girl! Speak up! Is it true or ain't it?"

This was too much to take in. Beth sank numbly onto a worn leather sofa. "Of course not," she managed to say. "I can't even imagine—why should such a rumour be spread about now? Surely had anyone believed such a thing, it would have been said before, and Chumley is dead."

"Well, someone did know, and someone's tongue has been loosened!" snapped her father. "You deny it, then?"

"Of course I do," said Beth. "I would never have done such a thing."

"What do you mean, would never have done?" Lord Fairchild smashed his fist down upon the scarred surface of his desk. "Did you or didn't you?"

"I certainly don't remember doing it," said Beth. "And I am sure that is because I didn't."

He stared at her in disbelief. "What namby-pamby talk is this?

Are you telling me you aren't sure of what you remember? Do you mean it could be true?"

"No." Beth wished her voice wouldn't quaver so. She was certain she hadn't done such a shocking thing. Indeed, Louis Chumley had held no fatal charms for her. But the truth was that she remembered so little about him that she suspected her memory was still faulty in this regard. "On my honour, father, I would never have done such a thing."

"It is your honour that concerns me!" he bellowed. "Very well. We shall have the doctor in."

It took a moment for his meaning to register. "You mean I'm to be pawed over like a prize pig, and all London is to be informed of the results?"

"Consider it how you will, it must be done." Her father, clearly relieved at having this unpleasant interview come to an end, strode toward the door to usher her out.

But Beth remained where she sat. "I refuse," she told him, "Everyone will say the doctor was bribed. The very fact of our going to such lengths will be taken as proof that the accusation is true."

The viscount turned to glare at her. "Then I'll call in three doctors. Or half a dozen, if you wish. No one could believe all of them would lie!"

"Oh, I like that!" Beth stormed to her feet. "I'm to be treated . . . to be looked at . . . to have all those men . . . it's worse than what they accuse me of! I won't have it, Father, I won't!"

For a moment their gazes locked. Beth knew her parent wished this matter disposed of, and would take the least troublesome course. That is precisely what he did.

"You shall return to the country," he said. "You shall never find a husband now, in any case."

And just to be sure the conversation was truly at an end, he walked out of his own study and left her standing there.

Tears spilled over and coursed down Beth's cheeks. What had she done to merit such treatment? Who would have spread such a horrid tale about her, and why?

For a dreadful moment, her suspicions fell on the marquis himself. He blamed her for his friend's death. Perhaps this was his revenge.

But why now? And why such cruelty?

The door opened again and Lady Fairchild came in, Hester trailing only a few steps behind.

"Well?" demanded her mother. "William has gone to his club without saying a word to me. What has transpired?"

"What do you think has happened?" cried Beth. "I'm to be sent to the country, and my name sullied permanently, with no way to defend myself!"

She pushed past them and ran up the stairs, barely reaching her room before a fit of weeping swept over her. Afterwards, she lay there in defeat.

The hounds had caught the fox at last. She had fought so hard, tried all her twists and turns, but in the end it had availed her nothing. How she despised them, all of them, and most especially the Marquis of Meridan!

Hester and Lady Fairchild, meanwhile, were discussing how best to salvage what was left of the season.

"I scarcely care," Hester declared when her mother asked how she thought they should proceed. "Sir Percy will follow her wherever she goes and offer for her. Then she'll be settled happily, while her reputation will continue to wreck my future!"

"Nonsense," said Lady Fairchild. "In a strange sort of way, this business may work to your advantage."

"How is that?" asked her daughter suspiciously as she followed her mother up the stairs to her sitting room.

"As it was, your father refused to send Elizabeth away," said Lady Fairchild. "Now she'll be gone. You are still quite lovely and, let us not forget, wealthy. Without her at hand to remind everyone of the scandal, gentlemen will soon willingly forget all about it."

Hester sank into an upholstered chair with a petulant look her mother could not recall having seen before. "Yes, but she'll have Percy!"

"That pauper?" sniffed Lady Fairchild. "Never mind him. And don't frown so, dear. You'll spoil your complexion, and you must look well tonight."

"Tonight?" Inexperienced though she was in social matters, Hester knew it was perilous to venture out while the storm was still raging. "You can't mean I'm to go to that costume ball tonight?"

"We are both to go," said her mother. "You have a lovely costume and so have I. We're to explain that Beth has a sick headache. No one will dare say anything to our faces."

Hester mulled over this idea. She'd had enough taste at her come-out ball to know she didn't enjoy keeping a stiff upper lip. On the other hand, Sir Percy would almost certainly be there.

Perhaps, without Beth at hand, he would notice Hester. And if he believed this story about Louis Chumley—which Hester quite honestly did not, knowing of her sister's longstanding infatuation with Meridan—wouldn't he necessarily lose interest in Lizzie?

"Very well," she said at last. "I'll go. And I must say, it's about time Lizzie paid the piper. I've certainly been paying long enough!"

At that very moment, across Mayfair, the fashionable folk of London were conversing on that same topic. It was about time the high and mighty, much too successful, disturbingly direct Lady Elizabeth Fairchild were taken to task for her reprehensible conduct.

As old-fashioned wigs were lowered onto heads, and historical gowns of heavy silks and velvets were laced up, the ladies of London turned over and over this delicious rumour. Had she really done that with Louis Chumley? And in the garden, of all places?

Sir Percy did not believe a word of it, and regretted only that it was too late in the evening for him to pay a call on the Fairchilds and express his support. He, like Beth, wondered who would have disseminated such a story, and why, and how anyone could believe that such a tale would come to light when one of the principals was dead and the other obviously would never have referred to it.

As to the marquis, his reaction was one of swift and fierce anger. "I should have suspected such a thing," he told Sir Percy over dinner, ignoring his friend's protestations. "Chumley would scarcely have been misled by a few fluttering winks."

"Nonsense!" cried Sir Percy. "You cannot tell me you believe this faddle! Why . . ."

The marquis's expression hardened. "You are being a fool, dear friend, but let us not argue. Shall we order more port?"

Since neither wished to quarrel, both relinquished the subject, but not before the marquis noted how vehemently his friend sprang to Lady Beth's defense. How like Chumley the young fellow was, he reflected bitterly, easily taken in by a clever minx and quick to believe the best of her in spite of everything.

He had been a fool to consider letting her intrude into his friendship with Mrs. Singleton. Beth's intense brown eyes, her independent spirit, and her honesty had impressed him deeply, but now they were once again proved false.

And, although he bore Ariadne no great love and knew she was far from flawless herself, she suited him in many respects. She had no girlish illusions about the married state; she was not given to temperament or unpredictable behaviour. And she was damned attractive.

It was time he took himself a wife and had an heir, thought Lord Meridan as he tooled his phaeton home to prepare for the ball. And Ariadne Singleton was the woman he had decided upon.

=13=

THE HOUSE IN Clarence Square had been transformed into a setting for a Greek drama. The walls were hung with cloths depicting olive groves and a distant Mount Olympus; arbours twined with real roses set off small glades filled with potted herbs and ferns.

As things Greek were all the rage, most of the guests had also chosen that era from which to draw their historical characters. Helens of Troy abounded, as did Platos and Socrateses, and, from the Roman era, Mark Antonies and Cleopatras.

Ariadne had dressed as Livia, haughty in a white gown and hung with turquoise jewellery that called attention to the aquamarine of her eyes. Lord Meridan, she noticed at once, had come as Alexander the Great, and looked magnificent in a silk toga and scarlet robe with an olive wreath in his hair.

No court of ancient times could have been more filled with gossip than was this one. Each time the butler stepped forth to announce a new arrival, all heads turned in case it might be Lady Elizabeth, and an audible gasp went up when her mother and sister were announced.

As was her duty, Ariadne came forward to greet them, having chosen to bypass the custom of meeting her guests as the entrance. Lord Winston had clearly expected to play host, and this had been the only means she could devise of getting around that little difficulty.

"I'm so glad you could come!" she cried, clasping Lady Fairchild's hands in hers. "Oh, and how lovely you do look! You are two ladies from the court of King Arthur, are you not?"

"She's Guenevere and I'm Lynette," said Hester impatiently, her gaze roving about the room. The chit looked entirely too appealing with her fair hair and blue eyes, but her sister's disgrace should keep her well within bounds.

"Lady Beth isn't with you?" Ariadne assumed a distressed expression. "But she helped me plan the ball!"

"I'm afraid she has the megrims," said Lady Fairchild, a bit too quickly. "She sends her deepest regrets."

The orchestra began a minuet, which Ariadne had chosen as just far enough old-fashioned to sound historical, and she excused herself—only to find Lord Winston waiting at her side.

He looked quite absurd, dressed as Julius Caesar, the robes hanging limply on his callow figure. Ariadne bit her lip as she allowed him to lead her out in the dance.

"Will they be gone by three in the morning, do you think?" he whispered as she pirouetted beneath his uplifted hand. "My horses will be ready."

"Oh, I hardly think so early," she grumbled. "Not before dawn, surely."

He frowned. "But that will be most inconvenient. We shall both be exhausted."

"Indeed." The figure of the dance separated them, and Ariadne fought to gain control of her annoyance. Could the fool not see that she no longer wished to marry him? No, she must make matters plainer.

As soon as the dance ended, she instructed him to escort her out of the ballroom on the pretext of checking to be sure the courses for supper were being properly prepared.

Once in the hallway, she turned upon him, considering her words carefully. Lord Meridan had not yet danced with her, and he certainly had not offered for her. Therefore she did not wish to burn her bridges quite yet.

"I fear we may have been imprudent in setting this evening for our departure," she murmured, looking at the viscount from beneath her deep lashes.

"But Ariadne, dearest, I . . . I would that we had left even sooner!" he blurted. "Everything is in readiness. Surely you cannot mean to delay . . . to delay . . ."

Annoyed by his stammering, she found her tone sharpening

"That is precisely what I mean. As you point out, we shall both be exhausted. Furthermore, as it may already be daylight, we might be seen."

"Fie on what people may say!" he proclaimed much too loudly. "We could be in Gretna—"

Unable to think of a more subtle way to stop his words, which might all too easily be overheard, Ariadne clamped a hand over his mouth, feeling it work wetly against her palm for a moment before desisting.

"There is no romance in a daytime elopement," she said firmly. "It shall have to wait for another night."

"Tomorrow then," he said as she removed her hand.

Ariadne shook her head in irritation. "No. La Catalani is performing at the Opera House, and everyone will be there. Perhaps next week. We will speak of this later."

"But when?" the viscount called after her plaintively as Ariadne turned back toward the ballroom.

"In the morning," she called. "Or the afternoon. Perhaps you could call upon me." And she hurried away.

To her vast relief, she saw the marquis heading toward her, wearing a determined expression. He bowed over her hand and requested the next dance, which she readily promised.

It was a country dance, and far too lively to permit any real conversation, but he did have time to convey that he wished to speak with her alone later that evening, if it were convenient.

Her heart beating more rapidly, she assured him that it would be.

But others were arriving, and so, when the dance ended, she was obliged to go and welcome a pouting Alicia Tonquin, fetchingly gowned as Juliet, and moments later a thoughtful Sir Percy Stem.

"Is Lady Beth here?" he inquired.

Ariadne shook her head and could not repress a short laugh. "How should she come, then?" she inquired. "Costumed as a certain woman of Babylon, perhaps?"

"I was thinking more along the lines of Joan of Arc," he said coldly.

Ariadne would not have been so gay at that moment could she have heard the conversation taking place in one of her rose-strewn bowers.

Lord Meridan, having little taste that evening for idle chatter, had secluded himself there only to discover a demoralised Viscount Winston.

He had been about to turn away when the younger man called softly, "I say, Lord Meridan, could I have your ear for a moment?"

"But of course." His lordship seated himself politely on a delicate white bench and sipped at his port.

"You know a good deal more of the world than I," began the viscount hesitantly. "Perhaps you could explain to me why women behave the way they do."

"If I could do that, I should be wealthy beyond belief," said Meridan. "But pray go on."

"There is a certain young lady . . ." began Winston. "Well, she has promised herself to me. Not publicly, you see. But we were to . . . well, may I be frank?"

"Of course." The marquis found his curiosity getting the better of him.

"We were to elope," said the younger man. "To Gretna Green and all that. Said she adored me, or something of the sort."

His suspicions aroused, Meridan frowned, but only nodded to his companion to continue.

"Now, on the very point of our departure, she puts me off," the viscount said. "Paltry excuses—the timing is not convenient, and so forth. I think she tires of me, but she will not say so. And why should she change her mind, in only a week's time?"

"Led you on, did she?" asked the marquis grimly. "Gave you expectations?"

"More than that!" exclaimed Winston. "Promised to marry me straight out."

"And now she leads you a merry dance." Meridan shook his head in disbelief. "How many men has she made fools of this way?"

"Beg pardon?" The viscount looked even more distressed. "You sound as if you know of which lady I speak, yet I have not named her."

"It is Lady Elizabeth Fairchild, is it not?" demanded the marquis.

"Why, no." Winston blushed. "My friendship with her is, uh

not of the romantic sort. No, it was of Mrs. Singleton I was speaking."

For once in his life, the marquis was left speechless. "Ariadne?" he asked at last, in a croak.

The younger man nodded. "Promised to marry me a week ago. We were to elope to Gretna Green tonight. And then suddenly she's changed her mind. I can't work it out at all."

But his companion was too lost in thought to pay much heed to the young lover's woes.

If Ariadne had promised to marry the viscount, she must have meant to do so. Since she had never flagged in her attentions to the marquis, he saw now, it was toward himself she had been playing some game.

Unexpectedly, he recalled what Beth had told him the night of her sister's come-out. Ariadne's first reaction to learning of his impoverishment had been to suspect him of trying to marry her for her money.

Perhaps she had plotted some revenge. But why should she change her mind now?

"I suspect Mrs. Singleton rather enjoys displaying her power over men," the marquis told the still distraught viscount. "Don't feel too badly, my friend. You're among good company. But you would be well advised to look about for a woman less changeable in her affections. Do not brood on this matter. Take action and look elsewhere."

Excusing himself, the marquis went out into the ballroom to look for his hostess. He still planned his conversation with her in private, but now it was to be of a considerably different nature. She had some explaining to do.

So distracted was he that he almost collided with the portly Lady Smythe, who greeted him effusively.

"You are looking quite well!" she exclaimed. "And not at all the poor fellow they would have me believe!"

"I beg your pardon?" he said.

"Mrs. Singleton was telling me only yesterday some bit of gossip she had heard about your losing at your investments," crowed Lady Smythe. "I set her straight, of course. It was because of your advice that I'm able to afford this." She spun about girlishly to display her golden gown, sewn with hundreds of seed pearls and trimmed with little chains of real gold.

"Glad to be of service," muttered his lordship, who was forced to endure several more minutes of her chatter before he was able to bow himself away.

Now, he reflected, he had the other half of the picture. Yesterday, Ariadne had learned that he was still wealthy. No wonder she had given poor Winston such short shrift. And to think the marquis had been on the point of offering for the mercenary creature!

A fury filled him, so great he thought he must smash his hand into the wall, and only a lifetime of propriety enabled him to restrain his impulses. Damn that Ariadne Singleton! She was another one like Lady Beth, all tricks and scheming and ways to twist a man around her finger!

He happened at that moment to catch his hostess's gaze upon him. Determined to spite her in whatever way he could, he seized upon the first attractive young lady he saw—Alicia Tonquin, as it happened—and invited her to waltz with him.

He was rewarded by the sight of Ariadne's mouth tightening grimly. Then the swift music caught him and he had to concentrate on the dance to keep from running into the other couples.

Although a passable dancer, Alicia showed no particular spark, and had the annoying habit of constantly gazing about her, as if seeking someone.

"If you tell me who it is, perhaps I can locate him for you," offered the marquis.

"What?" She looked up at him, startled. "Who who is?"

"Whoever you're looking for."

She blushed becomingly. "I do beg your pardon. I suppose I was being rude."

"Only a little."

"I hadn't meant to be." Alicia's habitual pout softened. "It's just that I'm worried. It's John, you see. John Winston. He's been hanging about in Ariadne's pockets, and I don't think she's good for him. Do you?"

"I don't think you need worry any longer," the marquis assured her. "Whatever plans she had for him I think are all spoilt now. If

154

you like, when this dance is over, I'll show you where I last saw him.''

For a moment the young girl hesitated. "He might not want to see me," she said.

The marquis shook his head. "I believe your interest would be most welcome just now."

True to his word, as soon as the music ceased he guided her to the bower in which John Winston still sat meditating upon life's cruelties. And there he left them to mend their differences and perhaps begin, on both sides, a more mature friendship than either had known before.

Even the marquis's dislike of Lady Elizabeth had been over-shadowed this evening by Ariadne's treachery, and the marquis almost wished Beth were present so he could dance with her and infuriate his hostess.

Since that was not possible, he chose the next best step—he danced with her sister.

However, he observed that Hester seemed inflicted with the same disease as Alicia, looking always here and there in the ballroom. In this case, he quickly determined that the object of her attention was none other than his friend Percy.

So Percy's strategem had worked, he thought with some satisfaction. But it was odd that Percy seemed almost oblivious to Hester now. Had he changed his mind, then?

"And how are you enjoying your first season?" he asked by way of making conversation.

Hester dimpled prettily. "It's been just lovely," she said sweetly. "Everyone is so kind and . . ." Her voice trailed off as Sir Percy whispered something into the ear of his dancing partner and both were swept into gales of laughter.

"And?" inquired the marquis.

Hester gazed up at him dolefully. "I hate it!" she cried. "Every minute of it. For years I've thought of nothing but what a splendid time I should have in London, and it's been just awful. And all because of Beth!"

"It does seem unfortunate that her actions should reflect upon you," he admitted. "I hope she will not wreck your season entirely."

"Oh, she will," returned Hester bitterly. "Even though father's sending her up to the country in disgrace. For all the difference that will make!"

The marquis regarded her in some confusion. "If she's to be sent away, surely that will remove the problem."

"Oh, indeed!" said Hester. "And what of Sir Percy? He'll only follow her, you know."

This bit of news did not please the marquis at all. Oddly, he felt a bolt of anger at the thought of his friend taking Beth into his arms. But he told himself his fury was because of the deception she was no doubt practising on his besotted comrade.

"I had not realised you held Sir Percy in such esteem," Meridan said as they danced. "A man of such indifferent means can surely not offer the style of life to which you are accustomed."

"So I thought once too," Hester admitted. "But I am not so enamoured of balls and gowns as I once was. The people are so petty—look at how they laugh in their sleeves at my having come tonight, when I've done nothing wrong! I don't care two shakes for them and their society. It's Percy I . . ." She caught herself barely in time. "Percy is not like that."

"No, he is not." Here the music ended, and the marquis bowed and went to collar his friend.

"Now there's a face like thunder," said Sir Percy as he approached. "Whatever can be the matter?"

Brett directed him out onto the balcony for a smoke, and the two were quiet for some moments as they prepared their cigars and puffed quietly. It was a balmy May night, as romantic as one could wish, with an almost full moon and a sky full of stars.

The sort of night when one should be out on the balcony with a beautiful woman, thought the marquis, and an image came to his mind unbidden: Beth in the orangerie, her auburn hair slightly askew, her eyes bright, her arms twining about his neck as he held her.

"Damn!" he said aloud, and Sir Percy raised an eyebrow quizzically. "Women!"

"Ah, yes." His friend nodded sagely. "Since Lady Beth is not here, may I presume the trouble falls with our esteemed hostess?"

"You may," said the marquis. "I was on the very brink of offering for her, when what does Lord Winston tell me but that she had promised to elope with him—only to break it off at the last moment. And do you know why?''

He continued without waiting for an answer, ''She had found out I hadn't lost my money after all. Now she's all sweetness to me and coldness to him.'' Despite the warmth of the evening, he shuddered. ''To think how close I came to being leg-shackled to *that*!''

Again the two men puffed for a while in silence.

''That was the purpose of our game after all, was it not?'' observed Sir Percy. ''To learn what others really think of us? So now you know.''

''Barely in time,'' grunted his friend, reluctant to concede the point. ''And by the by, you will find interesting what Lady Hester told me. It seems she's rather fixed on you, and has grown tired of gowns and balls. Or so she says.''

''Pity.'' Sir Percy stared regretfully at the glowing end of his cigar. ''I should have liked to marry her . . . at one time.''

The marquis stared at him in disbelief. ''Do you mean you have offered for someone else?''

Percy shook his head. ''Not yet. But I shall.''

''May I ask who?''

''Lady Beth.'' Sir Percy did not bother to regard his friend, knowing full well that he would see shock and perhaps even anger writ across his face.

''Beth?'' snapped the marquis. ''I can scarce believe my ears. After what she did to Chumley? And with Chumley, I might add!''

Percy turned on him angrily. ''You're like all the others, then, Brett. Every whisper of scandal finds its home in your mind. Can you not see the girl for what she is? She's everything that's decent and honest!''

It was true, of course, Percy thought. What he could not say was that, much as he liked and admired her, he did not love her. He would always love Hester. But she would easily find another suitor, and Beth would not. Beth would be relegated to old maidhood, stuck away in the country until her brave nature shriveled for lack of love.

He could not allow it to happen. He was her friend; he had even courted her, although they both knew that had been a sham. Beth might yet turn him down, but he would insist. Percy knew he could never be happy with Hester, knowing how mistreated and abused her sister was, and that he had allowed it.

But no one else need know the true state of his feelings. Let Brett think that love had entered in. It could do no harm.

"I can see it's no use arguing with you," Lord Meridan said grimly. "If you'll excuse me." Grinding his cigar out beneath his foot, he strode away.

He could not permit this misalliance, the marquis told himself as he crossed the ballroom. He had lost one friend because of that scheming wench; now he had the chance to save a second, and he would.

Courtesy required that he take his leave of Ariadne. Her eyes widened in dismay as he mouthed excuses for his early departure.

"But we haven't had our talk!" she protested. "Surely you needn't go quite so soon."

"Another time," he murmured, restrained by the presence of others from expressing himself more directly. "Good night, madam."

And he was gone, leaving Ariadne with her fists clenched tightly. So that was how he intended to treat her! It was a good thing she had not dismissed the viscount entirely.

It was in search of that young man that she went then, with no luck until she ventured to look into some of the private corners and bowers. After disturbing half a dozen sets of young lovers, she was about to withdraw in defeat when she spotted Lord Winston and Alicia Tonquin emerging through a rose-covered arbor, hand in hand.

As Ariadne glared in furious disbelief, the younger girl caught sight of her, and gave her one supremely triumphant smile before turning back to the viscount.

The evening had been a disaster of the highest magnitude. And Ariadne had not even Lady Elizabeth to blame for it.

=== 14 ===

LORD MERIDAN HALTED his phaeton in front of the Fairchild residence in Berkeley Square, leaping down and tossing the reins to his groom.

Only as he started up the steps did he remember that he was still costumed as Alexander the Great and must make a rather picturesque sight in his toga and robes. Nevertheless, he refused to delay this interview one moment longer, and so he rapped fiercely at the door.

A surprised butler answered, but quickly recovered his aplomb and ushered the marquis into the drawing room.

"I fear Lord Fairchild is at his club, and Lady Fairchild and Lady Hester have gone out," said the butler. "There is only Lady Elizabeth at home."

"That is who I have come to see," said Meridan brusquely. "Please bring her here at once."

The butler hesitated for only a brief instant and then, as if deciding to leave the matter in the hands of his mistress, left the room.

Angrily, Lord Meridan paced across the Persian carpet. This was the vixen who had wrecked Chumley's life, had flung away all decency and showed no shame at all. He'd be damned if he'd let her sink her claws into Percy!

Lady Beth's prompt appearance at the door, however, caught him off balance. She looked half-asleep, her reddish-brown hair falling freely about her shoulders and her brown eyes soft and puzzled.

A simple blue cambric gown clung softly to her slender figure, and for a moment the marquis stared at her, almost forgetting why he had come.

"I beg your pardon," said Elizabeth at last. "I was reading in my sitting room and I fear I must have dozed. Have you been offered any refreshment?"

"I do not care for anything, thank you," replied his lordship, finding it harder to begin than he had expected.

"I see," His hostess perched on the edge of a dainty parlour chair and regarded him with curiosity.

She should not have come down alone, the marquis thought, leaning against the mantel. It wasn't proper for her to see him unchaperoned even in the daytime, and certainly not at night with her parents away. But clearly such things had little meaning for Lady Beth.

As if following his thoughts, she said quickly, "I didn't wish to wake my maid. She'll be roused at dawn when Mother and Hester come home, and I thought it kinder to let her sleep. I trust your purpose here is of some urgency."

She stopped then, and frowned, her delicate face creasing in sudden concern. "No one has been hurt, I hope? There's not been a carriage accident?"

"No, no, nothing of that kind." Meridan shook his head. Now that he was here face to face with her, he found himself feeling unaccountably awkward. "I assure you, no one shall know that you came unaccompanied. I would never wish to sully your reputation."

Beth shrugged, and her mouth quirked with a bitterness he'd never seen there before. "Have you not heard? I've no reputation left to protect. I might as well behave as a wanton; I've gained no credit for behaving as I ought. But that's neither here nor there, my lord. Pray proceed."

What had got into him? Meridan wondered. His anger had disappeared in a tangle of bright hair and the gaze of a pair of sleepy eyes. Uncomfortably, he turned to a side table and poured himself a glass of claret.

Most women would have begun to fuss then, he realised; they

would have pressed cakes on him, or insisted the butler be sent to bring some fine wine from the cellar. But Beth merely sat quietly, regarding him as if quite certain that he would come to the point soon enough.

"In fact, I am here on account of Percy," his lordship began.

"He sent you?"

"No, not precisely." The marquis wondered how he had ever got himself to this pass. He had meant to confront her angrily, but now she was all calm reason and he felt more than a little foolish. "I understand—may I be frank, Lady Beth?"

"You have never been anything else," she said, "and I certainly do not know how to be otherwise. So please do."

"Percy has indicated to me that he intends to seek your hand in marriage," he said.

"Rubbish!" She clapped her hand over her mouth, then lowered it sheepishly. "Do forgive me, my lord. It's just that . . . he wouldn't. I mean, he doesn't love me."

"I believe you are mistaken," he said. "He has indicated the opposite to me this very night."

"But what of Hester?"

"He holds her in high esteem," said Meridan. "But it is you he wishes to marry."

"I cannot believe you are his emissary," Beth exclaimed. "But no, you said he didn't send you. Go on."

"I believe marriage between the two of you would be a grave mistake." He held her gaze firmly as he said it.

Beth studied him for a moment, colour rising to her cheeks. "Indeed?" she said tautly. "Why is that?"

"You do not love him," said the marquis. When she made no comment, he continued. "And you are not suitable for him. Percy is a kind man, and a gentle one. Although in some respects he is worldly, in others he is quite naive."

"Easy prey for an unscrupulous wench?" she asked with a dangerous edge to her voice.

"You mistake my meaning." He tried to quell her with a cold stare, but Lady Beth had never been meek-spirited.

"So you wish to warn me off!" She continued sitting, but her

161

back straightened and her chin came up in a familiar gesture that sent an unexpected tremor through him. "I'm unfit for your friend, am I? No doubt you believe every word they say about me—that I'm a ruined woman, that I led Louis Chumley down the path to his death. And now you fear I mean to do the same with poor Percy."

"Tell me then that you love him!" he demanded. "That you would follow him anywhere, live in poverty with him if need be! Assure me of that, Lady Beth, and believe me, I shall trouble you no more."

"Of course I do not love him," she said.

Despite all he knew of her, her boldness caught him off guard. "You dare . . . you dare to admit this to me!" He fought back an urge to pull the small, tense figure off the sofa and shake her. "That you have intentionally misled him, tricked him into loving you . . ."

"Bosh!" She stood up and faced him, sparks of anger lending a golden glow to her eyes. "If I do not love Percy, neither does he love me. Do you think I don't know that he only pretended to court me to make my sister jealous?"

"That may have been so at the start," he said, wishing the soft light from several branches of candles did not play so alluringly across her gently curving figure. "But I assure you it is no longer true."

"Did Sir Percy actually tell you that he loves me?" she asked, her tone quieter.

He had to reflect carefully before answering. "Not in so many words. But he said that he intended to marry you."

"Did he say why?"

His temper exploded again at her trickery. "What subtlety is this? Why else should a man wed a woman? It can scarcely be your money, when I assume your sister has the same portion."

"The same portion of money, perhaps, but not of misfortune," Beth said. "You say your friend is kind. Then why can you not see what he is doing?"

The marquis stared at her in disbelief. "You think he intends to marry you out of pity?"

Beth cocked her head in an unconsciously appealing manner as she thought over his question. "Not precisely," she said at last. "But I believe he is motivated by concern for me, not love. I assure you, he loves Hester and always will."

"And you would have him?" his lordship demanded, moving closer. "You would still marry him, merely for your own convenience?"

"Nonsense." Beth gazed at him with mingled scorn and dismay. "How very little you know me. Of course I shall not marry him. But then, I suppose, either way you shall think me a heartless wench."

"I beg your pardon?" The warmth of her nearness had brought back his earlier confusion.

"If I were to marry him, you would be sure it was only from selfishness," she said. "And if I refuse him, you will be sure I am cold and cruel, and led him along shamelessly just as you think I did with Mr. Chumley."

"Tell me the truth, then," Meridan said, hoping suddenly that she would at last defend herself. "What did happen between you and Chumley? If these things everyone says about you are false, then deny them!"

"How can I?" Her eyes clouded with tears. "I can't remember, Lord Meridan, I can't honestly. What I recall of him is so little—a few words here and there, a dance or so. It can't possibly be all there was. But I swear before God that I remember nothing else."

Oddly, he found he believed her. But what difference did it make? The fact that she did not remember could not make her innocent.

Yet as she stared plaintively up at him, he found himself drawn toward her, his hands reaching out to grip her shoulders, pulling her toward him. And she came willingly, shyly at first, and then with a great sigh as she curved her face up toward his.

He enfolded her, revelling in the softness of her mouth, the pliant yielding of her body against his muscular chest. Through her thin dress and his unaccustomed light robes, he could feel her heart pounding as she returned his kisses passionately.

The marquis slid onto the sofa, pulling Beth onto his lap and luxuriating in the feel of her thick hair falling around him. Still she made no objection to his caresses; indeed, she stroked his chest and his cheek, then moaned softly as he trailed kisses down her neck toward the inviting swell of her bosom.

It came to him that she would not resist him, that the gentle candlelight, the lateness of the hour, and her own fiery nature had driven away all thought of propriety. For a moment, his hands encircling her small waist, he was tempted to yield to his own hunger.

"Brett?" She seemed to use his Christian name unthinkingly as she blinked up at him, silently asking why he had stopped his advances.

As if dawn had broken in an instant, the marquis saw clearly how close he had come to falling into the trap he had thought set for Percy.

With a low growl, he pushed her off his lap and onto the sofa and stood up, glaring at her furiously. "So it's true!" he said. "You did disgrace yourself with Louis! Before tonight, I never truly saw how wanton you are. You hide it well, Lady Beth, but not well enough to trap me with your wiles."

For a moment she sat motionless where he had tossed her, regarding him with a puzzled, hurt look. Then she sat up slowly, a look of shame crossing her face, only to be replaced almost immediately by cold fury.

"If there's anyone who should level accusations, it is I!" she told him. "You come here late in the evening, knowing my family is away, and attempt to seduce me."

"I see." He stared at her icily. "Now you intend to report this interlude to your father, who no doubt will call me out unless I marry you."

Lady Beth shook her head, and the marquis experienced a tinge of regret as the rich, bright hair fell across her intense face. "Marry you?" she managed at last. "Not if you were the last man on earth! Now I must ask you to leave, Lord Meridan."

Something held him back. He told himself it was suspicion. Surely this scheming woman had no intention of quietly slipping away from London into solitary exile.

"May I ask what your plans are?" he said.

"My plans?" She frowned in perplexity. "I fear I do not understand, my lord."

"I came here to discuss Sir Percy," he reminded her. "I wish to know what you intend to do."

She squared her shoulders, chin high once more. "Very well. What I intend to do is to retire to the country, as my father has ordered."

"Oh?" He raised one eyebrow dubiously. "No more balls and gowns, Lady Elizabeth? No more handsome suitors, or rides in Hyde Park? You can hardly expect me to believe that."

"Yet you would readily have believed that I plotted to entrap you into marriage?" she queried.

It was his turn to experience confusion. "I do not see that the two things are incompatible."

"Then you don't plan to retire to Cornwall?" she asked.

The marquis caught his breath sharply, and scrutinised her face for any sign of irony or deception. Yet she seemed honestly not to know.

"The rumours regarding my financial situation have been disproved," he said.

"But it was Sir Percy himself . . ." She stopped, then continued. "A tale, then? To what purpose? Ah, I see. To test your friends. And were you successful?"

The marquis was feeling more and more uncomfortable. If she hadn't known the truth, then her willingness to accept his caresses might have some more noble—or at least more human—motive than he had assumed.

"In some regards, yes," he replied cautiously.

"Mrs. Singleton seems not to have altered her behaviour toward you," she observed.

He felt himself flushing angrily at the thought. "We were not discussing Mrs. Singleton, and pray leave her out of this discussion."

Their eyes met, and in hers he read an undisguised pain that surprised him.

"I see," she murmured at last. "Well, I believe we have said quite enough to each other, my lord. Please excuse me. The hour is late, and I leave for the country tomorrow."

Without waiting for his reply, she nodded briefly and swept out of the room, leaving behind a faint trace of perfume and the image of untamed hair floating above a slender, vulnerable back.

The marquis stood motionless for several minutes. She had misunderstood about Ariadne, mistaken his anger as a defense of that blasted woman.

Could Percy have been right about Lady Beth? Was she really the soul of honesty, and had her willingness to surrender to him truly come despite the belief that he had lost the better part of his fortune?

Deeply troubled, the marquis let himself out of the house. The butler was nowhere to be seen.

Yet, he reminded himself as he took up the reins of his phaeton and headed away through the glistening dark streets, there was still the matter of Louis Chumley.

He must have been right in his appraisal of Lady Beth. He only wished she were not quite so enchanting with her hair undone, nor quite so irresistible when she clung to him and matched his desire with her own.

What a fool I am, falling under her spell in spite of everything! he told himself angrily, cracking his whip to spur the horses onward. Let Percy have the confounded woman! Thank heaven that's the last I'll see of her this season.

And he urged the horses faster still, as if hoping to outrun the pain that squeezed at his heart.

=15=

Although the sun was shining and the birds did their best to bring freshness into the streets and courtyards of London, Sir Percy Stem awoke with a leaden feeling of impending doom.

He had sworn to Meridan at last night's ball that he would marry Elizabeth Fairchild, and marry her he would.

Despite his laggard spirit, Sir Percy ordered his valet to dress him in his best coat of dark green superfine, a striped waistcoat, and buff coloured trousers, with only a single pearl in the folds of his snowy neckcloth. It would not do for Lord Fairchild to think him a fop.

In his newly repaired phaeton, Sir Percy made his way to Berkeley Square. What an odd turn of events this was, he reflected as he drove through the late morning bustle. It was Hester he loved, with her bright blue eyes and fair hair, and it was to her house he rode, but to marry another.

Then he thought of Beth, of her honest gaze that glinted with pain and loneliness. He could not abandon her. His fellow members of society had treated her cruelly, and he would never be content to let it pass.

Fortified by these thoughts, Sir Percy drew up before the Fairchilds' house and descended. Yes, the butler said, Lord Fairchild was in his study.

Moments later, the two men were shaking hands and the viscount was offering Sir Percy a glass of port, which he declined, and a seat, which he accepted.

It was the first time Percy had ever asked for a young lady's hand in marriage and he could not repress the faint hope that his lordship would refuse. But no, he told himself sternly, that must not happen.

"If I may be direct," he began.

"By all means, by all means." Lord Fairchild nodded vigorously, as if eager to have the interview done with.

"I've come to request the hand of your daughter Elizabeth in marriage," said Percy.

The older gentleman frowned thoughtfully. Clearly this was an unexpected turn of events. "There are certain facts of which you should be aware . . ." he began.

"If you are referring to the slanderous tales spread about your daughter, I do not credit them in the least," Sir Percy assured him.

"Quite. Quite." The viscount sank down behind his desk and tapped one finger on the surface. "And then, forgive me, but there is the matter of how she is to be supported."

"Oh, yes. As it happens, I have just come into quite a bit of money." Sir Percy outlined his changed situation rapidly and saw the creases ease from the other man's face.

"Then there can be no objection, of course," said his lordship. "It is done. We shall have the marriage contract drawn up at once."

"Er . . . Haven't you omitted one thing?" suggested Sir Percy.

The viscount considered. "I don't think so," he said. "To what are you referring?"

"Your daughter's consent."

"Oh, that." Lord Fairchild snorted. "Naturally, she will agree."

"Nevertheless, for the sake of the formalities . . ."

"Oh, very well," said his host, and rang for a servant to summon Lady Elizabeth.

She received Percy in the morning room, the sunlight bringing out the red highlights of her hair. She looked quite lovely, save for the dark circles under her eyes and the pale, haunted look she wore.

"Lady Beth, are you unwell?" asked Percy as he bent over her hand.

"Merely tired," she said, her voice unaccustomedly quiet. "I have been packing. I am to depart for the country just after lunch."

"Indeed, I hope not." Sir Percy looked at her awkwardly. Now what the deuce was a chap supposed to do? Ah, yes, there was some business about getting down on one's knees and doing it up proper.

Therefore he lowered himself uncomfortably onto his knees, thankful that the Persian carpet would not soil his trousers. "My dearest Lady Beth . . ."

"Oh, do get up, Percy!" she exclaimed, reaching over and tugging at his sleeve.

"I will not!" he retorted. "Now I have got down here, I am not going to get up and explain and then go through this whole business all over again."

"But I don't want you to go through it at all."

"Unreasonable chit!" he exclaimed. "Do sit quietly for once and let me get on with it."

"But you are about to propose marriage!" she protested.

"Well, of course I am!" said Sir Percy. "I'm not such a pauper as you think, Lady Beth. I say, do give me time and I shall explain myself."

"But I know about it. Lord Meridan came last night to warn me off!"

Percy looked up in shock. "He did what? Blast that fellow, I'll call him out!"

"You'll do nothing of the sort. He was entirely right." She reached down and helped Sir Percy to his feet. "Besides, I have no intention of marrying you. You're in love with my sister."

Percy dusted himself off, wondering what had become of his dignity. Here he had finally got up his nerve to carry the thing off, only to find himself hauled about and reproved in the most outrageous manner.

"I don't suppose Meridan offered to marry you himself, did he?" he asked suspiciously.

She shook her head. "Of course not. Everyone knows he's in love with Ariadne Singleton. But he thought I was setting some sort of trap for you." She cut off his protest with a raised hand. "Oh, you and I both know that isn't true. But we also know that you love Hester and you only want to marry me out of pity, or sympathy, anyway."

"And a strong sense of justice!" said Sir Percy.

"Well, I'll have none of it." Beth sat down on a Chippendale chair and poured them each a cup of coffee, thrusting one into his hand over his protests. "I'll not be married to a man who loves someone else, no matter how good friends we are. So you are just going to have to marry Hester."

His injured pride calming somewhat as he realised that he was almost out of danger, Percy said, "But what of you? Stuck away in Kent, a beautiful young woman done in by lies and gossip. How can I be a party to that?"

"You shall stay here and tell everyone of my noble character," said Lady Beth with a quirk of a smile. "Your assurances will outlive the gossip and perhaps someday I may return. At any rate, I won't have you, and that's that."

They sipped their coffee in silence for a moment before the door was flung open and Hester flounced in, her hair flying disordered about her exquisite face and her eyes flashing blue lightning.

"So!" she cried. "Father tells me you're to be wed! I suppose you're proud of yourself, Beth, having snatched him from under my nose! And you, Percy . . ." But before she could go any further, the tears overflowed and she turned to dash away.

Slamming down his coffee cup with a force that nearly shattered it, Sir Percy ran to catch her by the shoulders. "Your father was wrong," he said. "It's you I love. I proposed to Beth from a sense of honour, as she well knew, and she has turned me down. And now, if you'll have me, Hester . . ."

She turned to stare up at him in disbelief. "You really . . . you do mean that, Percy? You're not just angry at Beth?"

"What devil has got into this household?" he demanded as he caught her in his arms. "Am I to be forever throwing myself on my knees and uttering protestations? Are my motives to be eternally questioned? I have asked you to marry me, woman, and I await your answer."

"Yes!" cried Hester, throwing her arms around him. "Yes, yes, yes!"

In the delirium of actually holding her and sharing her kiss, Percy was not aware when Beth slipped from the room. Then things seemed to happen quickly. There was Lady Fairchild to be told, and Lord Fairchild, who scratched his head and muttered something about becoming partially deaf in his old age.

"For some reason, I had the impression you wished to marry

Elizabeth . . . but never mind," he said. "Happiness, good luck, and all that. Off to my club now." And he went.

Finally Sir Percy took leave of his delighted fiancée and her faintly pleased mother. Now that he had revealed the true state of his finances to Lord Fairchild, he had certain matters to square away.

Abraham Meyer was in the habit of conducting his business from the Stock Exchange Coffee House in Threadneedle Street, where he might learn the latest news of trade and ships and so make the wisest possible investments.

It was here that Sir Percy found him at noon time, reading a newspaper he quickly laid aside at the nobleman's approach.

"Good morning, Sir Percy," said Mr. Meyer, a balding gentleman of middle years whose jovial expression hid a quick mind. "In need of more funds, are we?" For Mr. Meyer's capital was made by the time-honoured business of loaning money—for a consideration—to down-on-their-luck gentlemen.

"Quite the opposite, in fact." Sir Percy sat down but declined a cup of coffee. "I have come to pay you back." He produced a note from his man of business. "You may redeem this for all that I owe you. I have come into some funds, you see, Mr. Meyer, and shall not be needing your services again, or so I hope."

The other man nodded, his expression revealing nothing as he accepted the note. "Congratulations, Sir Percy," he said. "I would that all my clients should have such good fortune."

Percy glanced about him at the traders and businessmen crowded about the tables, heatedly discussing the latest news of the Royal Exchange. "In a way, I'll miss all this," he admitted. "There was always the hope, you see, that somehow I'd strike it rich myself, find a wealthy wife or get lucky at gambling. Now that I've inherited in such a stodgy fashion, all the fun has gone out of it. I've even found myself a wife with a respectable portion, when I'd far rather have rescued her out of poverty or had her rescue me. So unromantic, you know."

Mr. Meyer shook his head. "Young men are such dreamers," he said. "So was your friend, Mr. Chumley. Ah, you did not know he came to me? It was from me he borrowed his fare to America. I loaned it to him from pity. I knew I would never see it again, although I did not guess the tragedy that awaited him."

"Was he in so deep as that?" Percy said. "I knew he owed money, but I'm certain he'd have paid it back in time."

An indulgent smile crossed the other man's face. "You young men and your sense of honour. Paid it back? I doubt it. The only reason I do not lose my equanimity is because I had never loaned him much myself, knowing his propensity for gambling too deep. But there are always others wishing to take a chance—for a stiff consideration."

Percy found himself even more puzzled. "But gambling is common among all young bucks, you know. I've lost a pound or two in my time."

"But not fifty thousand of them," said Mr. Meyer.

A wagon rattled by, filled with boxes stamped in the name of some heathenish city in India. "Fifty thousand . . . ?" The words stuck in Sir Percy's throat. It was a fortune indeed. Far more than Louis Chumley could likely ever have repaid in his lifetime, even if he had married well.

"He was most distressed, of course," Mr. Meyer went on. "Had to get out of the country or he'd be thrown in the Fleet, you see. I took pity on the chap. Wouldn't do his lenders any good to have him in prison, now would it? I thought perhaps in a new country he could at least make a respectable life for himself."

The implication of his words was only beginning to sink through Percy's brain, befogged as it was with the day's unexpected twists and turns. "He was going to America to avoid debtor's prison?" he asked hoarsely.

Mr. Meyer nodded. "Sad thing, if you ask me. Someday they'll do away with that sorry business. Not that I want to see debtors get off easy, mind you, but what's the use of putting them away where they can't work?"

Another gentleman stopped by their table, a down-at-the-heels chap who evidently wished to approach Mr. Meyer on the delicate topic of money. Percy yielded his seat and departed.

So it was debts and not a broken heart that had driven Louis Chumley to that fatal ship. How then had the rumour begun that Beth was to blame?

Sir Percy was still mulling this turn of events over lunch at White's when he spotted Meridan entering across the room. A wave of the hand and his friend came to join him.

The marquis looked unaccustomedly solemn, Percy noted at once. "Still angry over that business with Mrs. Singleton?" he asked.

Brett shrugged. "Just congratulating myself on getting away in time." But he didn't look the least bit happy.

"Speaking of congratulating, you can do a bit of that with me," said Sir Percy. "I'm to be married."

To his utter consternation, his friend looked upon him with an expression that could only be described as severely unfriendly. "Indeed? And who is the fortunate young lady?"

"Hester Fairchild," said Percy, and was relieved to see Meridan's look soften.

"You are indeed to be congratulated," said the marquis. "May I ask what changed your mind about Lady Elizabeth?"

So that was it. His friend was in love, Percy thought, glad to have his suspicions confirmed. "She wouldn't have me," he said. "She knew perfectly well what I was about and wouldn't hold with it. By the by, she told me you'd been to see her, Meridan. Not very sporting, you know."

Brett's expression darkened. "And what did she say of my visit?"

"Only that you wanted to warn her off me," Percy assured him. "That reminds me. Had the devil of a discussion with my money-lender today."

"Oh?" They were interrupted by the waiter, from whom they ordered cold chicken and salad with green beans, and claret. After he departed, the marquis asked, "Thought you were done with that business."

"Went to pay off my debts," said Percy. "Abraham Meyer —you wouldn't know him, by any chance?"

Meridan shook his head.

"Shrewd fellow. But kind-hearted. Lent Chumley his passage to America, as a matter of fact." He waited for a reaction, but his friend sat regarding him silently. "Knew he wouldn't get it back, he said."

"Something of a mystic, is he?"

"No, no, indeed." Sir Percy answered. "Nothing of the sort. Hadn't an inkling of what was to come, but it seems our friend owed a bit more than we might have guessed."

"Oh?" Lord Meridan still showed no especial interest as the claret arrived and he poured himself a glass.

"In the neighborhood of fifty thousand pounds," said Sir Percy.

The marquis choked on his drink and had to be slapped on the back. "Good Lord, Percy! Fifty thousand—that's a bloody fortune!"

"Exactly so," said Percy. "Seems he told our friend Meyer he had to get out of England or he'd be thrown in the Fleet. Now what do you make of that?"

"Nonsense." Brett seemed to have recovered, although his voice still had a strangled sound to it. "Everyone knows he left because of Lady Beth. Told me so himself."

"Oh?" This was getting to the heart of the matter. "Precisely what did he say?"

"Well . . ." Lord Meridan's eyes half-closed in concentration. "Said he'd fallen in love with the wrong woman, had his heart broken, and thought he'd try his luck in the New World."

"Did he mention anything about Lady Beth in particular?"

Again, his friend thought carefully. "No, not that I can recall."

"Then how did her name come into it?" Sir Percy leaned across the table eagerly.

"Blast if I know. Common knowledge, I guess." But Lord Meridan sounded less sure of himself than ever before. "It was well-known he'd been courting her."

"For her money, it was reported at the time," said Percy. "And what about this rumour, her bestowing her favours on Chumley in the garden and all that? How does this manage to turn up almost a year after he's gone to a watery grave? Where's it been hiding all this time, then? Or could it be someone just invented it?"

"Who would do such a thing? And who'd believe them?" But the marquis was clearly troubled.

The waiter set their luncheon before them. For a time the two men ate in silence.

"Something damn smoky about it if you ask me," said Sir Percy. "You know what I think?"

"What?"

"Sounds like the kind of thing a jealous woman would come up with. Someone who wanted Lady Beth out of her way."

Lord Meridan mulled the thought. "I can't believe . . . Percy, if this is true, then I've wronged her. Wronged her terribly." A dark shadow seemed to have fallen across his face. "I would almost rather it were true, than that I had been so unjust. And to her of all people."

It was as close to an admission of love as Percy could have hoped for. "We'd better follow it to the end, then, don't you think?" he asked, his own spirit lightening. If he indeed could be the means of clearing Lady Beth's name, then he'd have done all she asked—and have no reason to feel guilt about his wedding to Lady Hester.

There the matter stood for the time being. A jealous woman, but who? Had there been someone in love with Chumley who resented his interest in Beth? Or had there been some other man who had unwittingly inspired such cruel falsehoods?

Those questions were still rattling around in Lord Meridan's head the next night when he went to the opera. Afterwards, he could never remember who had sung, or who he had seen, except for Alicia Tonquin and her family.

Restless, he was strolling about at the interval and chanced to notice them sitting in their box. Alicia looked up at that moment and gestured to him eagerly through the half-opened curtains.

Unable to ignore such an obvious summons, his lordship entered and made the required pleasant chitchat for several minutes before Alicia's parents had their attention drawn away by other visitors.

"I only wanted to thank you!" cried the young girl. "It's not been announced yet, but John and I are to be married, and it's all thanks to you!"

"I hardly think so," demurred the marquis. "I'm not in the habit of matchmaking."

"More of making magic, I should say," replied the dark-haired young lady, her eyes sparkling. "You freed him from the wicked witch."

"I beg your pardon?"

She giggled. "Mrs. Singleton. She'd cast a spell upon him. Something you said during your little tete-a-tete must have cleared his head, and then you showed me where he was. I don't know how to thank you!"

"I'm afraid you give me more credit than I deserve," he responded, rather uncomfortable at this outpouring of girlish admiration. "It was she herself who showed her true colours. He'd already begun coming to his senses."

She shook her head. "You've no idea how devious she can be. The very next day, well, he tells me she tried to renew their friendship, or whatever you might call it. Actually went to call upon him at his rooms, to apologise for her behaviour! But it was too late. If not for you, he might have taken her back. Oh, she's a clever one, but she's lost this time!"

The music resumed and Lord Meridan was able to escape to his seat, but the pieces of the puzzle were beginning to fall into place. Ariadne. Scheming, devious Ariadne.

He tried to remember. Who had first told him that Lady Beth was the one with whom Chumley was enamoured?

The memories began creeping back. He had been put off somewhat by Lady Beth's hoydenish ways, but attracted in spite of himself. Uncomfortably aware that she might ensnare his heart before he was certain he wished to be attached, he had carefully avoided her.

At the time, Ariadne had been his mistress. She sensed, of course, that he was slipping away, although he had no intention at the time of leaving her convenient bed. Perhaps she had seen his surreptitious glances at Elizabeth . . . .

The news of Chumley's death had come in late summer, just as he was about to leave for Kent. Did Ariadne know how near the Fairchild estate was to his own?

He recalled berating himself for not preventing Chumley from leaving, and Ariadne attempting to reassure him. It had not been his fault. Someone had broken Chumley's heart and he must get away.

Yes, it had been Ariadne. Although he could not remember the exact words, suddenly he was sure of it. It was she who had told him that Beth had teased and deceived the young man until he was quite mad with grief.

The rumour of their supposed intimacy—when had that come? Just before the masked ball, at about the time Ariadne learned that the marquis was not impoverished. Had that too been a stratagem to dispose of an unwanted rival?

But this was all unfounded speculation. Chumley had courted Lady Beth; she had admitted as much herself. And she confessed she still could not recall details of their acquaintance. It would not do to convict Ariadne Singleton without evidence.

He must confront her, thought the marquis. The next morning, he would face her and learn the truth.

=16=

SO FAR THAT morning, Ariadne Singleton had discharged one maid —a poor country lass with nowhere to go—and smashed a dish, scolded the cook for overcooking the eggs, and become so enraged at finding a wrinkle in the first dress she donned that she ripped the garment to shreds.

So John Winston was to marry that encroaching little chit Alicia Tonquin, and someday make her his duchess! It was enough to drive a mortal soul wild.

And then there was the business of Lord Meridan, Ariadne reflected as she flipped irritably through a stack of invitations in her sitting room. At her ball, he had been all attentiveness at first. Surely his mention of needing to speak to her in private had implied that he meant to ask for her hand in marriage!

Then with no explanation he had fled, abandoning her. Surely it had been evident to all her guests that Mrs. Singleton had no man at her beck and call, no anguished admirer hanging about her skirts. And why? Lady Beth had not even been present, so she could scarcely serve as a scapegoat.

Slowly Ariadne sank through clouds of annoyance to a semi-substantial earth. It was of no use to sit here brooding. She must find a way to discover what had disturbed the marquis, and set it right.

Surely Providence was on her side, for only a moment later, her butler came to announce that the marquis himself was at this moment downstairs awaiting her.

"The drawing room, please, and offer him refreshment!" commanded Ariadne, with a quick glance at the pile of curls atop her head and the seductive decolletage of her powder blue morning dress. What man could resist that? Brett certainly hadn't tried to in the past.

Feeling more confident by the moment, she sauntered down to the drawing room, posing briefly in the doorway to be sure he received the full effect of her figure and face. Then she settled beside him on the sofa, wishing he were not quite so inscrutable. Had he come to offer for her at last? She felt her heart pound so loudly that surely he must hear.

"I've come on a rather delicate mission," said Lord Meridan, watching her closely.

Ariadne lowered her eyelashes demurely. "I shall do my best to be of service, my lord," she murmured.

"It concerns Louis Chumley."

She hesitated. His words were ambiguous. "Yes?" she asked, trying in vain to read his mood.

"It seems his statements of having had his heart broken were somewhat exaggerated," continued his lordship. "Did you know he owed fifty thousand pounds? That he fled to avoid being thrown into debtor's prison?"

Ariadne's mind raced, trying to see around the corners of his statements. "I knew he had debts, of course," she hedged.

Brett leaned back on the sofa, his long legs stretched before him easily, and she felt a bit comforted. He would scarcely make himself so at home were he about to accuse her of spreading falsehoods.

"Did he confide in you?" asked the marquis.

She shrugged. "Perhaps a bit. We were old friends, you know."

"He told me once the two of you had been lovers," his lordship said conversationally. "Said you were the only woman he felt he could unburden himself to. He must have mentioned something of this."

There was no point in denying it, and besides, her visitor did not seem perturbed by the thought. "Yes, that's quite true," said Ariadne. "Of course we were merely friends by the time you and I became involved, you know."

"Of course."

He waited expectantly, so she added, "He did confide in me

about his feelings for Lady Elizabeth, but I was shocked when they became common knowledge. Naturally he had sworn me to secrecy. But it was quite true.''

"Then he must also have told you about their . . . intimate relationship,'' suggested the marquis.

Ariadne fought down an urge to squirm. If she denied it, that would be tantamount to saying the story was untrue. In that case, she would undo her own revenge and perhaps even encourage Meridan to marry the wench. "Well, yes,'' she said finally.

"The topic seems unpleasant to you."

"Only because I was shocked when it got about,'' said Ariadne with a calculated touch of self-righteousness. "I had not realised he had told anyone else, but clearly he did, and they had not my scruples.''

Her handsome visitor continued reclining against the arm of the sofa, an ironic expression playing across his emerald eyes as if he had just perceived something amusing. "How convenient,'' he muttered, half to himself.

"I beg your pardon?''

"Lady Smythe,'' he said. "It was she who disabused you of the notion that I had become impoverished, was it not? I wonder I did not see this before. Naturally, as she is the biggest gossip in London, one would need only to tell her a choice tidbit to have to spread across town by the next evening.''

"I don't know what you're implying!'' snapped Ariadne. "Impoverished? Nonsense. You're one of the wealthiest men in the country and always have been.''

"Odd.'' He sat up, leaning closer to her with one elbow resting on the back of the sofa. "At your ball the other night, Lady Smythe was laughing about some foolish notion you'd got, that I'd lost my money, and how she'd had to set you straight.''

"Interfering old witch!'' stormed Ariadne. "So she's been inventing tales about me, has she?''

"It won't wash, my dear,'' he said, still with that maddening calm that so disconcerted her. "Mrs. Smythe may be a gossip, but she isn't malicious. And then there was that business about running off with John Winston. Rather hard on the boy, weren't you? Promising to elope, then putting him off, then trying to win him back after I walked out on you. However, I must say, you'd have eaten him alive sooner or later.''

Ariadne glared at him wordlessly. Never in her nastiest dreams had she imagined that Lord Meridan would learn about all her schemes and make all the connections. How had he done this? Lady Beth . . . but even she couldn't have known about Lord Winston or Lady Smythe.

He must have become suspicious, or had a simple run of luck. His lordship, like many wealthy men, had always been fortunate at cards.

''You're a bloody fool, Brett Meridan!'' She stood abruptly and paced across the room. ''I won't even bother to contradict all these ugly lies you've put together about me.''

''You disappoint me,'' he said.

''But I will tell you this!'' She glared at him vengefully. ''Your sweet, innocent little Elizabeth is as cool a schemer as they come. She's the one who told me the lies about your losing your money— set me up, she did, right proper!''

A faint smile teased at the corners of his mouth. ''Not quite, my dear Ariadne. It was Percy who told her the story, and she believed him. We spread the tale on purpose, he and I. It fulfilled its purpose, wouldn't you say?''

She clenched her hands in rage. So she'd been caught in a trap after all, from the one schemer she'd never suspected—the marquis himself!

''Now what do you plan to do?'' she demanded in a low, dangerous tone. ''Spread this tale about London to discredit me? That would give you pleasure, I suppose.''

He stood to face her, his posture still relaxed. ''I take no pleasure in your downfall, Mrs. Singleton. Indeed, you do not need me to accomplish it. John Winston, as you've no doubt heard, is engaged, and so shall I be soon.''

''If she'll have you, after the way you've behaved!''

''That's between her and me,'' he said softly.

''Oh?'' Having glimpsed his weakness, Ariadne launched her attack. ''Yes, perhaps she will. Sent to the country in disgrace, what choice does she have? But it will never be the same, you know, Brett. You've had no faith in her; she's been ill-used at your hands, almost as badly as at mine. She'll never be able to feel the love for you that you'll expect from your wife. Take it from another woman—no matter how much she wants to forgive, there'll always be a wall between you. And it was your doing, all of it, you and your stiff-necked intolerance! Well, go to her then, and may the devil keep you company!''

She stalked past him out of the room, but not before surreptitiously taking in the grim expression on his face.

Even before his carriage rattled away, Ariadne was ordering her maid, now reinstated, to pack up her things. She would spend the rest of the season in Bath.

Any scandal he spread about her would be forgotten in six months' time. But Lady Elizabeth, she suspected, would never forget.

The summer-green fields of Kent helped soothe the turmoil in Beth's heart as she rode out the next day.

She had refused to be attended by a groom. After all, what was there left of her reputation to lose? And she wanted to be alone just now.

A shady patch beneath a large, spreading tree beckoned to her, and Beth reined in Daisy, then slid down from the sidesaddle. How long ago it seemed that she had careened through this same countryside on another mare, only to be thrown upon her head.

Had that not happened, she reflected as she tied the reins to a bush so Daisy could graze, she might not be in this tangle. If only she could remember for certain what had passed between her and Louis Chumley . . . but it was too late to worry about that now.

Sinking down onto the grass, she pulled from her pocket the letter that had arrived only this morning by messenger from her father.

Squire Hanson, a beefy middle-aged widower and longtime crony of Lord Fairchild's, had requested Beth's hand in marriage. Even he had heard the rumours, but he was not dissuaded; in fact, that was no doubt what had given him the courage to ask.

He could make use of a young wife, for his pleasure and to be mother to his four children. And he could make use of her dowery also, Beth reflected. Not that the squire was a bad man. He was kind enough, she supposed, and the children she vaguely recalled as cheery apple-cheeked youngsters.

Against her will, she thought of the marquis, his tanned face bending over her, his arms seizing her and drawing her into an embrace. And then he thrust her away, swore that her passion for him proved she had granted even greater favours to Louis Chumley . . .

Angrily, Beth brushed away a tear. She would not weep for him From the very beginning, the man had despised and scorned her Nothing she could have done would have convinced him of her innocence.

Unconsciously, her hand had clenched around the letter, and now she withdrew the crumpled missive thoughtfully. She migh never have all that Mary did, but even without a husband one loved, there was much to be said for a quiet, respectable life in the country.

In time she would have children of her own. And never agai would she have to go to London, to face the lies and scandal against which she found herself so helpless.

Very well, she thought. I'll marry Squire Hanson and be don with it.

This decision made, she stood up and reached for the mare' reins, only to hesitate at the rhythmic pounding that signalled th arrival of another rider.

It must be one of the servants, come to fetch her, she thought a she paused.

The horse that galloped into view over a rise was far too fine stallion to be ridden by any servant at Fairchild House, and th rider's form too commanding to be anyone but the marquis.

An embarrassed flush spread across Beth's face. She must hav ridden onto his land without realising it. She had no idea why h would have come here from London, but a meeting with him wa the last thing she desired.

Untying the reins, she moved to mount Daisy. Unfortunately situating oneself in a sidesaddle was no mean feat and certainly no something she often attempted unaided. As a result, she foun herself clinging precariously to the saddle as the horse ambled on i way.

"Whoa, there!" Meridan spurred his stallion forward and leane to catch the reins. Daisy halted suddenly and Beth, off-balance, tumbled down, catching her ankle in the stirrup and twisting it as she fell.

"Lady Beth!" The marquis leaped to the ground and knelt beside her. "Are you all right?"

"I've twisted my ankle," she admitted, glad that a curtain of hair veiled most of her face. "If you'll be kind enough to summon one of my servants, I'll be off. I apologise if I've ridden onto your land, Lord Meridan."

"You haven't, and I shouldn't care if you had," he said. To her consternation, he remained kneeling beside her, reaching down to inspect the injured joint. "It's beginning to swell already. I can send for a carriage, but I don't like to leave you here. Are you up to riding behind me, do you think?"

She nodded, still keeping her face averted. It was an embarrassing business, being lifted in his strong arms onto the stallion's back, then clinging to his taut body as they rode.

The pain in her ankle, which despite her best efforts jounced against the horse's side, failed to dispel her confusion. Why was Lord Meridan home in the midst of the season? How had he found her, and why was he suddenly so solicitious? She gazed back at Daisy, being led behind them, but the contented mare provided no answers.

Indifferent as she was to her surroundings, it was not until the horses stopped and Beth looked up to see the turrets of a medieval castle that she realised Lord Meridan had brought her to his home instead of hers.

"My lord!" she protested as he dismounted and reached up, catching her about the waist. "I should not be here!"

"We shall convey you home by carriage as soon as you are rested," he assured her, his grasp setting off a warm rush that threatened to engulf her. "We were closer to my home than yours, and I wished to spare you as much pain as necessary."

Then you had far better left me where I was, she thought, but said nothing.

He scooped her up, carrying her past the startled servants and issuing orders as he strode through the house to the morning room. Her head pressed against his chest, Beth found herself distressed by memories of her stay here some months before. Then, she had still hoped that he might care for her. Now, she saw clearly that he was only behaving as a neighbour and a gentleman ought.

Mrs. Wakeham arrived as Beth was being lowered onto a settee, and clucked away to fetch tea and cakes.

"I'm dreadfully sorry to have put you to so much inconvenience," Beth told the marquis, who was arranging a comforter over her legs. "I seem to have a talent for casting myself into difficulties, don't I?"

A troubled look crossed his face and he straightened, pacing away from her to stand gazing out one of the floor-length windows over a green lawn.

"The trouble has not been entirely of your making, it seems," his voice floated back to her.

"I should have known better than to have tried to take London by storm," she protested, unable to restrain a trace of bitterness. "I belong in the country, and here I mean to stay."

"You're far too young to seclude yourself," he reproved, still not looking at her. "You should not resign yourself to withering away here."

"I don't intend to," Beth said with a firmness she was far from feeling. "My sister Mary is quite happy, living with her husband and children in the country, and so I intend to do."

He looked toward her then, the sunlight behind turning him into a dark silhouette. "I beg your pardon?"

She swallowed a lump in her throat. Perhaps once he knew that she was safely out of the way, at least the two of them need no longer be enemies. "I'm to be married. To Squire Hanson. So you see, everything has worked out for the best."

He stood motionless for a while, the breeze through an open window ruffling his hair and giving the only proof that he was not a statue.

Mrs. Wakeham returned at last with the tea and cakes, and made a great fuss adjusting the comforter on Beth's lap and serving her. It seemed hours before the woman went away.

"Is something wrong?" Beth asked when they were alone again.

The marquis sat stiffly in a straight-backed chair. "My best wishes to you both," he said. "You made no mention of this when last we met."

"It is . . . recent," she admitted, letting the hot tea soothe her parched throat. "It's not been announced yet."

His eyes caught hers. "Do you love him?" he asked quietly.

Beth coughed and set aside her tea cup. It was an unexpected and impertinent question. Any self-respecting young lady would reprove him for his insolence, or turn him aside with some diplomatic comment.

But Beth was only Beth, and all she could do was cry out in a choked voice. "Oh, don't ask me questions like that! What difference does it make if I love him?"

In an instant he had left his chair and was sitting beside her, his body bent over hers and his green eyes probing her brown ones. "All the difference in the world," he said. "Beth, I love you. I suppose I always have, but oh, how I fought it. Don't marry him, my darling. Marry me."

She couldn't believe he had really said those words. "I think . . . there's something wrong with my hearing," she gasped. "Or my brain. I thought you said . . ."

"I asked you to marry me."

She closed her eyes for a moment, expecting to wake and find herself at Fairchild House, or dozing in the grass. But he was still there when she looked up. To her amazement, she realised from the tension in his muscles that her answer meant a great deal to him.

"But . . . Chumley . . ." she said.

He shook his head. "It was lies, all of it. Ariadne Singleton spread them to keep us apart, and fool that I was, I believed it. There was nothing wrong with your memory; there was nothing to remember."

It took her a moment to absorb all this. "I hadn't lost my memory after all? About Chumley, I mean? Ariadne . . . she did all that? But you've always despised me anyway. Haven't you?"

By way of an answer, his mouth closed over hers. Beth had the sensation of falling, and reached up to anchor herself. The touch of her hands on his shoulders served only to bring them closer together and to her bewilderment she realised a moment later that he was stretched alongside her as they shared one lingering kiss after another.

With all her strength, Beth pushed him away and sat up wildly. "Is this another of your traps?" she cried. "Am I to be accused of some transgression, some lack of innocence because I allow you such liberties?" To her chagrin, tears streamed down her cheeks.

The marquis knelt before her, his hands cradling her face as he kissed the tears away. "Beth, Beth," he whispered. "Will you ever forgive me? What must I do to make you forget? Ariadne told me you'd never forgive me, that even if you married me, all our lives my coldness, my lack of faith would come between us. But I do love you, Beth. I want to marry you, no matter what the terms. Someday I'll prove that I can be trusted."

Unexpectedly, Beth found herself laughing. "I shall just have to ride Fancy again and arrange to have myself thrown on my head."

To his dumbfounded expression, she explained weakly, "So that I can forget everything, and then there will be nothing to come between us."

Now the marquis too was chuckling as he sat beside her again. "Then you will marry me?"

"Yes, I shall!"

If Mrs. Wakeham was surprised, on entering the room a few minutes later, to find her master passionately embracing Lady Elizabeth Fairchild, she gave no sign of it.

Indeed, her primary sensation as she tiptoed from the room was one of relief. It had been clear to her from the very beginning that this was the girl Lord Meridan should wed. It seemed to her that having to cast oneself off a horse twice for one gentleman was quite enough, and it was high time he came to his senses before the young lady suffered some permanent injury.